Paradise Smith

This is a story of love, hate, hope and despair—and of a man fighting to save the achievements of twenty-five years. Smith's world was the island, the mountain, the Paradise River. And his extraordinary little ship. His solitary life had grown from the years alone in the jungle fighting the Japanese, and one terrifying incident that had brought him back time and again to challenge the gorges and rapids that ringed the base of the mountain.

This self-imposed challenge was all but over when the mountain trembled and the lava flowed. Surviving the worst that nature could conjure up was nothing new to Smith. But now people were involved, two people, each strangely connected with his past. Ruth Carter, escaping from her own exile in the valley high on the mountain; and Blik, Smith's wartime protégé and now president of his new country. The author weaves together all the elements in this drama to achieve an unforgettable climax in the swirling waters of the estuary.

PARADISE SMITH

Ronald Johnston

COLLINS
St James's Place, London, 1972

William Collins Sons & Co Ltd
London · Glasgow · Sydney · Auckland
Toronto · Johannesburg

Set in Intertype Imprint
Made and Printed in Great Britain by
William Collins Sons & Co Ltd Glasgow

Chapter 1

The mountain had many names and as many legends. It was worshipped and hated. It gave life and took it away. It inspired good and attracted evil. It was a beautiful mountain. It was a terrifying mountain.

By day it dominated the length and breadth of the great island with the soaring sweep of its jungle clad sides and the sparkling whiteness of its snow cap, a constant surprise out there in mid-Pacific; by night its shape showed hugely against the tropic sky, cut off across that flat peak, its snow band gleaming in the crown of red light from the lava bubbling deep in the crater. The mountain's presence was not only visual. It spoke all the time, the gurgling of the lava lake carrying down the slopes on the swirling air currents, the rumbling of its volcanic heart vibrating through the tangle of ravines around its base. Occasionally the mountain would cough and spew out a column of fire and ash or the lava lake would well up and overflow the crater and cut a swathe down through the snow, then the jungle, to cool and become rock and soon be covered over with new snow and new jungle.

Smith knew all about the mountain. No European knew more. But he was never awed by its bulk or its majesty, never fearful of its voice or its spasms. For Smith, the mountain was just there. It had been there, in close or distant focus for thirty years. It had been a landmark, permanent, reassuring, through the years of being hunted and chased by the Japanese as he watched and noted and radioed back and moved on. After the war he had never got around to leaving the island. Not that he was specially welcome when the British and Dutch came back to take over their colonies. Wartime heroes are best fêted, decorated and sent home. They can get in the way of administrators. Bucking the powers-that-be was something Smith could never resist. So he had stayed. Anyway there was no one and nowhere to go back to. He was then still a young man, not yet thirty, but he had lived so long only for survival from one day to the next that he had none of the young man's view through the years ahead. But if Smith was an old man when still young, he had a huge zest for life. He did everything with the boundless enthusiasm of a child and survived by his veteran cunning and shrewdness.

He stood on the deck of his boat and stared across the pool at the black cliff. It was here, at the headwaters of the Paradise, that Smith felt at his best. All the elements of his world were here. The mountain, the cliff, the jungle, the river and, most of all, his beautiful, ridiculous little ship. He grinned. He was always excited at having beaten the river again. It was just the exhilaration of winning. It meant nothing to him that not even a native canoe ever penetrated that far up the Paradise. All the surveys marked the river as unnavigable from twenty miles farther down. Rightly so. No one in his right mind would have attempted to bring a boat up through the three long gorges and all the rapids beyond that point, never mind a boat like *Mermaid* that was really a ship.

That first time, a quarter of a century ago, he had left the boat below the gorges and hacked his way through the jungle. It was the secret he then discovered that made him blast ways through the gorges and make trip after trip up to where he now was. That secret was not the secret of why he had lived when he was sure he was about to die. The real secret of the cliff was something else. He often wondered about that drive to seek out the cliff. He wondered if, in that long fall towards death, some trick of light had

6

seared an image on his brain, an image forgotten but, from deep down in the mind's store of things seen and unremembered, giving birth to that hunger to find and explore the cliff. Smith knew he was not the first white man to reach the head of the river. Maybe they had portered round the rapids with canoes or small boats but they had been there a long, long time ago. He was there because they had been there. For other reasons too.

Mermaid was a hundred years old. She was long, with a sharp bow and a heavily raked yacht stem. Her sides ran out to a matronly beaminess midships which was held right aft to her rounded stern over a sharply cut-in counter. Her hull was almost all that remained of the original boat. It was of iron and seemed immune to time and weather. The only other original fitting was the funnel, thin, tall, shaped at the top like a bell askew. It was brass all the way. It was set right aft, giving the little ship an unbalanced look, only partly redeemed by the mast up front which carried the derrick for the cargo hold. The funnel was not necessary. The ancient boiler and steam engine had been replaced by two big diesels but Smith chose to run the exhausts up through the funnel. It was that funnel, tarnished almost black, poking up out of the water in a creek at Port Bancourt that had led Smith to his boat. He had a loyalty to things if not to people.

Gutting and refurbishing the boat had been Smith's main occupation for the first year after the war. Three years in the jungle had left their mark. The boat was his therapy. It became an obsession. He knew what he wanted. He wanted a boat that would be a home, a boat he could trade round the coast, a boat he could take up the Paradise River. She had been built as a coast and river yacht to carry Queen Victoria's colonial governors about their business. She had come a long way down in the world when Smith found her.

He used the island woods to restore her. He was good with wood. That was one of many arts the headhunters had taught him. It took him ten years to get the boat the way he wanted her. In that first refitting he had concentrated on essentials. He installed the engines, redecked her overall and built a deckhouse that served as bridge and cabin. He allowed himself only two indulgences. The funnel, lovingly burnished till it shone like a golden phallus; and a figure-head which gave the boat its new name. A mermaid, her head erect, hair streaming down over her shoulders, arms flung back under the turn of the bow, breasts straining forward, scaly tail clinging to the stem and just touching the water. The skin was gilt, the hair and nipples bronze, eyes green, lips orange and tail iridescent blue.

Smith stared at the cliff and listened to the sounds of the river and the birds and the squeaking of the tyre fenders against the rock shelf where *Mermaid* was moored. Familiar sounds, lulling sounds. He wiped the sweat from his face and walked along the deck. He had beaten the river again but he still had his routine to keep. The routine at day's end was to hose down fore and aft. Routine was important to Smith. He called it system. His day was as carefully organised as any monk's. It was the reason he was such a good survivor. It meant that his boat not only always looked good but that everything on it worked perfectly. It meant that he was always fit and sharp. He had learned about system when he went to sea. He had fought against it then because no one told him the why and wherefore. It was just there. It had always been there. You served the system. That was why society worked. If you bucked the system, you were an outcast. Smith chose to be an outcast. His system was personal. It served him, not the other way round. He had learned his why and wherefore the hard way, on the mountain and in the jungle. It was not the kind of war he had expected.

8

He had been at sea from the beginning, in the Atlantic. Then his ship came out to Australia and up into the Pacific just in time for Pearl Harbour. Early in '42 no one in Port Bancourt believed that the Japs would reach that far. But they did. They landed on a morning when Smith was waking up to a monumental hangover. It had been quite a party. He had met Pop Merritt in a bar. It had seemed a shame to stop so they hopped a plane and flew up to Pop's plantation. When they started to come to, the only planes in the island skies were Jap planes. Pop's transceiver told the story. Troops were ashore all along the north coast. It was going to be a short campaign. They abandoned the plantation and faded into the jungle and the caves and ravines round the mountain. The tribesmen hid them, fed them, guided them. The radio lasted out long enough to tell them that the island had been overrun and to make vague and unlikely arrangements for contacting those who had survived inland.

By the time someone in Australia remembered that promise, six months had passed and Smith was the only survivor. Pop Merritt had died and the handful of other planters and government people had been captured or picked off by patrols. Smith had not wasted his time. He had learned from the natives. He learned about the jungle from the black fuzzy-haired pygmies, about the river and the swamps from the tall brown skinned tribes there, about the mountain from the Pochaks, the strange pale people of the high valley. He learned and listened to the drums. In the end the drums told of the white man who had come from the sea. He was a Dutchman who had once been a district officer on the island. He took Smith down to the coast and they waited for the submarine to come back. There was enough gear for a small army. The American war effort was obviously getting into its stride. Smith took the radio, the guns, ammunition and explosives. He sent the Dutchman back with the chewing gum, the chocolate, the Lucky Strikes, the K rations, the magazines and the bundles of uniform clothing. Someone had forgotten to send any instructions for the equipment. The radio and the guns were not too difficult. With the explosives, Smith had to learn by trial and error. He was lucky and in the end he was a real artist.

From high on the mountain he had a clear view north-west towards the Philippines and south-west towards New-Guinea. His radio reported every Jap ship that moved on that vast stretch of ocean. But the Japs heard the radio too. They started chasing him. His little army killed a lot of them. The nearest they got to taking him was that time at the cliff where his boat now lay. They were clever. They had no paratroops and no helicopters. But they did have seaplanes. They packed two of them with troops and landed them on the lake high up on the mountain. They squeezed Smith from above, down towards their men coming round both flanks of the mountain. He buried the radio and told the men to disperse. Two dozen targets would slow up the Japs. He made for the river. He could hear the water as he came out of the trees. Ahead it was flat and rocky, just bushes and a tangle of ground creeper. Poor cover. He looked up. There was a light plane circling slowly, spotting. He waited till it was heading away and started running from rock to rock, bush to bush, running, crouching, crawling, stopping. He had covered a couple of hundred yards before he realised he had trapped himself. Ahead he could see a steep slope, dense with trees. But it was beyond the edge of the ground he was on. It was on the other side of the river and the edge of his ground was not a river bank. He was on top of one of the cliffs that fringed the river. He looked right and left for a way off and down. Then he heard the plane. It seemed small. It was pointed straight at him. He pushed himself down into the creeper. The engine noise grew then faded. He looked up. A red flare was drifting down above him. He ran, stumbling, slithering, for the edge of the cliff. It was his only chance. His breath sounded loud in his ears but there was also the noise of the plane and whistling and shouting from the trees behind. He flung himself down on the edge of the cliff. He could hear the river but he could not see it. He stretched out over the edge. He swore. That way was certain death. The top of the cliff swept out in an overhang. If he jumped he would crash to the far bank more than a hundred feet below. His hands searched over the edge but the rock was weathered smooth. A shot came from the trees on the mountain and the bullet swished overhead and to the right. That calmed him. If this was to be his last fight he would make it worth while. He knew the Japs too well to want to be taken alive. He crawled along the cliff edge to where the flatness of the ground was broken. It was a scatter of big boulders shrouded in creeper. He crept in between two which gave a clear view back across to the mountain. The soldiers were out of the trees, spread in a long line, bent low, moving slowly, searching. There was time. He checked his rifle. He wanted to make every bullet count. The plane was still circling. Smith grinned. You've lost me, you bastard. You can't see me with all this lovely creeper on top of me. The plane dropped lower. Smith shrank down, fingers and toes pressing into the ground, seeking invisibility. His left arm disappeared up to the shoulder. He lay and stared as the plane roared overhead and away. He rolled over and pulled out his arm. Pebbles ran over the edge into the hole. They were a long time dropping. He measured the distance of the troops. About a hundred and fifty yards but they were going more slowly now. He thrust his arm back into the hole under the angle of the big stone and felt around. Rock. And that was a ledge. He slipped out his jungle knife and struck at the ground to widen the hole. The noise sounded as if it would be heard a mile away. The ground broke away and rattled down into the shaft. The hole was still small, maybe eighteen inches across. He checked on the Japs. Not much more than a hundred yards now. Smith licked his lips. He was dead already so anything was worth a try. He slithered round and slid his legs down into the hole. It was tight over his hips but he wriggled them through. He stuck fast at his chest. If these Nips find me like this they'll really have fun. He heaved back against the stone. It gave a little. His feet searched out a firm hold and he strained back again. The stone moved and he got his chest half-way in. One more desperate heave and his shoulders were through. He reached a foot down. Yes, there was another ledge there. He pulled in his rifle and his machete and dragged the creeper down to screen the entrance. He took a deep breath. He realised he was still dead. They would find that hole for sure. They would fire down it, drop grenades down it. He swore. Better if I'd stayed up top. At least I'd have got some of them. Hell. A chance is a chance. How deep is this hole anyway? He holstered his knife and strapped his rifle across his back to free both hands. He found a hold and explored with his feet. Another ledge. It was smooth, unnatural. He lowered himself again. He shook his head in the darkness and sniffed the musty air. Faintly he heard whistles and shouts above. He seemed to hear the river too. It's a bad dream, he decided. I'm dead already. I'm wherever you go when you're dead. It's a black hole in the ground with slimy stone steps and you crawl backwards down them into eternity. It's easy. One leg down, other leg down, one hand down, other hand down. Down and down. But it was not easy. Half-way down the shaft he stepped confidently on to nothingness.

Smith stood on the deck of *Mermaid,* remembering. He

smiled. That fall had been one climax of a nightmare that dogged him through the rest of the war and the year after till he came back to lay the fear and discover the greater secret of that rock wall. Then the fear had gone and been replaced by the excitement of what he found. Not just excitement. For twenty-five years he had had the challenge of finishing what he then started. And the amusement, for it had turned out to be the richest joke in his life. He frowned. Tomorrow it would all be over. There would be no reason to come back. That was something he had known he would have to face some day. Now the day was almost here. He laughed out loud and the cliff caught the sound and flung it back at him. No problem. He could keep on coming back, turning back the clock, giving the cliff back its secret. He had to come back. It was the place most like what other men called home, the place you remembered when you were not there, the place your family came from. Smith had no family but it was here he had found the boy who had become a sort of son. He was still holding the deck hose in his hand. He turned it on himself and the cool water gushed over his head, making him splutter and gasp for breath. It had been like that the day he fell.

He was never sure if he had cried out. It only took seconds but it stayed in his mind as a slow and terrifying lifetime. That cold clutch at his guts as his right foot stepped down and found nothing. The fear gripping his throat as his body heeled over and lost contact with the walls of the shaft. The hopeless inevitability of his fingers clawing on the smooth slimy stone and finding no hold. Then, as if in slow motion, his body turning as it fell, his eyes seeming to see light where there was only darkness, his brain parading a flurry of distorted, irrelevant images. The sudden certainty of death and the prayer that it be painless. Then the cold shock of contact, unbelievably yielding, the sudden relief at survival, the returning panic as he sank through the water and was held and dragged on and down by new and unseen hands. The bruising touch of rock, the thunder in his ears, the crushing pressure on his chest. Endless torture. Then light, and air rushing into his lungs but no respite. Dragged on, turned, twisted, bruised, beaten, sunk, surfaced, suffocated, succoured, hounded by noise, hopeless with terror, carried headlong towards death so recently escaped. Suddenly at rest, abatement, oblivion and a cradle of soothing, painless light and shade. A sort of paradise.

Smith fought against returning reality. He tried to put away the pain flooding back into his body, not to hear the sounds of the real world, not to see the person taking shape above him. It was a vague shape but growing ever more solid, leaning down to him, stretching out to strike. He knew that the face would be oriental, topped by a soft, high-crowned, small-peaked cap. He knew that outstretched arm would hold a rifle. He wondered if it was turned butt down to smash on to his face or bayonet down to slice into his belly. Quick, please, just make it quick. And final. Fingers trailed across his forehead, caressed his cheek. Fool. You're already dead and it's just like Omar Khayyam. An endless prospect of gorgeous girlies. No. That's too easy. That's what you're supposed to think. They want you to relax, stop fighting, gather your strength. Then they'll start. They'll ask questions, they'll threaten, they'll cajole. They'll beat you to the ground and kick you and piss on you and make you crawl like an insect. They'll revive you, give you water, a cigarette, smile at you. Then they'll cut and pierce and twist and hammer till your body is a horrible heap on the ground. But they won't let you die because they must make you talk. They need to know where the radio is, where the codebooks are, what the call signs are, what the schedule is, who your tribesmen are, where your stores are hidden. They'll keep you alive till you tell them. Then

14

they'll check and if you lied they'll come back and it will all start again; if you didn't lie they'll come back and gleefully nail you to a tree and parade in proper military fashion then charge at you to polish up their bayonet drill. And just before you die they'll take you down from the tree and chop your head off with a sword. Oh Christ.

He opened his eyes wide. The boy was young, nine, maybe ten years old. He had straight black hair, pale brown skin and startlingly blue eyes. Smith's mouth dropped open. A little hand covered it at once and the blue eyes frowned him to silence. He closed his eyes and opened them again. It was real. He tried to make his eyes tell the child he understood. The hand was taken away from his mouth, hesitantly. Smith smiled his thanks. His face hurt. He tried to move his body on the ground. Every muscle protested. He let his head fall to one side, then the other, to broaden his view. The river was there, rushing past just inches away. Across the water reared a sheer wall of rock. He followed it up with his eyes. He wondered if it was the same cliff he had come from. His eyes searched along the top for any sign of soldiers. Nothing. He looked round at where he lay. He was on a piece of rock in a gash in the river bank. There was thick scrub jungle all around but through it he could see cliffs on his side. He was in a gorge. He had never been there before—he didn't like gorges, too easy to get trapped—but he knew roughly where he was. The gorges ran for miles and miles round the base of the mountain, guiding the river down to where it broke free and widened and slowed and began its long meander through the swamps to the sea. The boy was standing now, unravelling a net. He smiled shyly and made a mime to show Smith how he had been caught in the net and pulled ashore. The boy's head came erect and slowly turned with the grace and acuteness of a wild animal. He nodded and smiled; he was satisfied there were no soldiers. He stretched out a small hand, gave a quick bow and said, 'Blik.'

Smith took the hand and held it as he struggled to sit up. He was confused. *'Blik?'*

'Goed verstann, mynheer. Doet het pyn?'

Smith frowned. Pyn? Of course. Pain. Dutch. The blue eyes, the pale skin. Native mother, Dutch father. All the planters had their mistresses. And some brought up the kids as their own. But there were no Dutchmen left. They had all been taken or killed. The small hand was growing hot in his. He shook it firmly and nodded his head. 'Smithy.'

'Smiddy?'

'That'll do well enough.'

And so it had been all through the years. It still was though now there was no contact, no communion. In his maudlin moments Smith could convince himself it would change in time, that it would be as it used to be. But he knew it never could be. Blik was an important man now. President of his new country, trying to weld a nation from a hotchpotch of Micronesians, Melanesians and Polynesians, not to mention Chinese, Malays, Javanese and an inheritance of half-castes like himself. And for all that variety they numbered barely a hundred thousand. But in the crazy world Smith turned his back on, Blik had his place at the United Nations and was making a mark in world politics. His charm, good looks, wit and beautiful English made him a welcome guest at diplomatic parties. But he was the current darling of the big Pacific powers only because his half of the island was where it was.

Smith swore and turned off the deck hose. He shook himself like a dog and spat over the side. You're a silly old goat, Smithy. You're like all the other petulant parents in the world. You tried to mould a child into the kind of person you wanted it to be and you get all huffy when the kid turns out to be a human being with a will of his own. You're

16

cynical enough about human beings and human relation-
ships. You should have expected that. All kids hate their
parents at some stage. Sometimes for ever, other times just
till they start to understand. True, but not all sons promise
to kill their fathers. I'll grant you that but all fathers aren't
like you and Blik did say he'd wait till the right time came,
if it came. He's a very straight man in his own way, Smithy.
That's something you did teach him. He'll wait till he's got
a good case for killing you. He has your beautiful old-
fashioned manners. That's rich. You and I know he'd think
he had a great case already, over there in that cliff, if only
he knew about it. I'm almost tempted to let him know
except that that would spoil the other thing and that's more
important. Are you sure about that? I'm too wise to be
sure about anything. Except routine. I'm sure about that
and the routine now is that I shave and change and have a
drink and eat.

He stayed at the table after his meal and smoked a cigar.
That was part of the routine. It let him think about the day
past and the day coming. It was enjoyment and relaxation.
His evening meal was a formal affair. The food was carefully cooked, the table in the saloon properly laid. He sat
at the head of the table from where he could view the nine
empty places, four each side and one at the far end. His
dress was formal too. Not the dinner jacket or tails of the
cartoonist's English colonial though the idea was the same.
Smith wore a brightly coloured cotton wrapper from waist
to ankle in the native fashion and a white silk shirt, open
necked and short sleeved. The saloon was built on the
main deck of *Mermaid* with big square windows down each
side. It was the central part of the long deckhouse that
started with the bridge and wheelhouse and ended with the
galley just forward of the funnel. Between the saloon and
the wheelhouse was a sitting-room with built-in settees
round three sides, the bulkheads above them lined with

book-packed shelves. Against the fourth bulkhead was a writing table. This was Smith's den. He usually slept there or outside in a hammock. The proper sleeping cabins were down below in the hull. There were four of them, each two berth, two to port, two to starboard, served by a companionway from the saloon. Aft of them and running the full width of the engine room bulkhead was a bathroom with showers and basins and WC's. These cabins had been built to let Smith carry occasional passengers round the coast or up the river. He did not like other boats on his river so he took government staff from both halves of the island on their infrequent trips. The cabins were now proving a money spinner in his new venture of hunting the salt water crocodiles which infested the mudbanks of the estuary. It was remarkable how much American and Australian businessmen would pay for a week on *Mermaid* and the promise of at least one crocodile.

The other cabin had its own stairway. It was used infrequently but always memorably. It was big, the full breadth of the boat, with its own spacious bathroom across the fore end. Bath with shower, vanitory unit, WC, bidet. In the cabin the deck was covered in thick carpet. There was a dressing-table, built-in wardrobes with fitted drawers. There was wall lighting, mirrors and some good pictures. The cabin was dominated by an immense four-poster bed. An envious wit had described that part of *Mermaid* as the mistress suite.

Smith smoked his cigar and stared out of the saloon windows. It was dark now and the evening rain had just stopped. The lights from the ship reflected in the river and drew shadows on the cliff. He chided himself for wallowing in all these memories but he told himself it was temporary. They were always in sharp focus up here at the head of the river. Maybe more so this time because this was the last time. It would make no difference if he came back again.

This would always truly be the last time. He knew it was like any other end, not an end but just a new beginning. And whatever was begun would be exciting, a challenge, absorbing, rewarding, because that was how Smith was. But eventually it would go sour and disappoint. He wondered if that too was because of how he was. He chuckled and stubbed out his cigar. Life was helluva funny.

His hand stopped over the ashtray. He frowned. The sound of the drums was faint but unmistakable. Smith went out on deck and listened. These were the drums of the river people, the sound funnelled miraculously up to him through the gorges. The drums spoke of the mountain. The mountain was angry. The mountain was going to punish them. They had offended the mountain. They were leaving their villages. That was odd. The river people worshipped the mountain but never suffered from its spasms. Their problem was flash floods. The boat shuddered in sympathy with some vibration deep in the rock. Smith was erect, tensed, listening. There were more drums now, nearer. From the jungle tribes round the base of the mountain. That made more sense. The boat shook again. If there was going to be a lava flow, it was the jungle people who would be in danger. But they knew how to handle it. They would move out, wait and watch. If the lava did not reach their villages, they'd go back. If their villages were destroyed, they'd build new ones in new places. But why should the river tribes be leaving? That worried Smith. To be caught in the gorges in a flash flood could mean the end of him and his boat. He looked up at the sky. It was clear and star filled. Not a cloud anywhere. But there was something. The overhang of the cliff was etched against the sky, a sky pink from some hidden source of light. Lava. That must be it. *Mermaid* shuddered again. Smith stared at the cliff. If that lot breaks loose, I've had it. Just have to hope. Can't do a thing in the dark. I wouldn't get out of this pool never mind down through the gorges. What am I worried about? It's only a lava flow. I've seen plenty of them. All right, I know, I'm worried about these drums from the river. I trust the tribes and, most of all, I trust the river tribes.

He went in and got the binoculars and checked and slung a rifle. He flung off his shirt and dragged up the cotton skirt between his legs, tucking the end in at the waist. He had to know more about what the mountain was doing. He went ashore and started up the long slope. He seldom used the torch. The glowing sky and his instinct guided his feet. It was the same slope he had looked at from the top of the cliff that day he was running from the Japs. There were no trees now, just scrub and creeper. He had demolished all the trees, blowing them down with well judged charges, stripping them, logging them, dragging them down and winching them aboard *Mermaid*. They had been superb hardwoods. Some of them were now part of the boat. The others he had got high prices for in Port Bancourt. It was a long climb but he knew that from the top he would have a clear view above the cliff.

He gasped as he turned. The mountain was incandescent. He put up the glasses and tracked left to right. The snow band was intact. The fire and light started lower down. It was as if a furnace had been tapped and molten steel was pouring out in a great flood, unrestricted, spreading out and down, consuming everything in its path. Smith lowered the glasses and rubbed at his eyes, already sore with the glare. The mountain seemed to have split open from side to side and was letting its lava core drain out. That was crazy. He put up the glasses again. It started to make sense as he spotted the sources. One, two, three, four. It looked like four holes in the mountain with the lava gushing out, spreading as it oozed downwards, firing the scrub and trees, the flames rushing hungrily in search of new fuel, fanned by the fickle mountain winds, leaping the gaps between the

20

lava flows till the whole side of the mountain high up was a sea of fire. The Pochaks will get it first in that secret valley of theirs. They won't have run away. They'll survive. They've survived up there for a thousand years. Maybe more than that. These big gullies will run the lava clear of their valley.

He lowered the glasses and blinked his eyes. Just a lava flow. A big one certainly. But what about these drums from down the river? Have the old men misread the signs? Or can they see beyond the lava and the burning mountain to some greater danger? Smith shrugged. Old men. Nothing to be done till dawn in any event.

He looked down the slope to the river and the glowing lights of *Mermaid*. We'll survive. Like always. We'll maybe even have time in the morning to finish that job we came to do.

Chapter 2

They stood half-way up the steep southern slope of the great valley high on the mountain, watching the slow tide of fire flooding towards them. They were strung out in family knots, old men and women to tiny children, the whole little nation of the Pochaks. They stood and stared, fascinated, awed, but with no sign of fear. The mountain was their mother and would do them no harm. She would speak and scold but only to remind them. She would weep for them with tears of fire until their father, the sun, who did not weep because he was a man, returned and ate up the darkness and dried the tears and comforted his woman, the mountain.

It was as the wise one, Manutami, had said when he came back down into the valley from the high place where the wise ones listened to the mountain. This was to be the testing time of the strangers. The mother mountain had tired of their presence. If their gods were so strong, let them quench her tears of fire with the magic words in the strange tongue. The mountain would judge the strangers as she had judged these other strangers in the dim past of the Pochaks. Then too the strangers had told of a strange man-god who spoke of poverty and death. And the strangers made the Pochaks bring to them all the tears of the sun which they harvested from the great lake for these, the strangers said, were riches and without them the Pochaks would be poor and better able to meet the man-god. The Pochaks had not understood for their riches were pigs and yams and children. But they obeyed because the

22

mountain made no sign. When they had brought the strangers all their store of the tears of the sun, the strangers called them liars and beat them and touched them with fire to make them tell where they had hidden their riches. Then the sun, their father, spoke to the Pochaks. He told them he would weep no more for his tears had brought them great trouble. He told them they must never travel to the lake again but must wait till all the strangers but one fell ill with a strange sickness and could not speak and fell to the ground and died. Then the stranger who had not been stricken should be put on the long water and sent to tell his people that the sun and the mountain were stronger than their man-god, and the dead strangers should be put in the place where they kept the tears of the sun and the place should be sealed forever and be known to all the Pochaks as a forbidden place. When that was done the sun told the Pochaks to climb the mountain and there they would find a place to build their houses and plant their crops and rear their children. So the Pochaks climbed the mountain and found the valley and knew that this was the place for the mountain their mother roared and shook and threw away her peak like a woman slashing the nipple from her breast and poured out milk of fire and the fire covered the mountain but did not come into the valley.

The Pochaks stood and watched the flowing lava. They watched the two strangers, man and woman, and thought ahead to the test. Manutami had said that the fire would flow down into the valley for the first time in their long history and the man stranger must turn it back. The Pochaks stood and watched their mountain on fire, feeling the heat and smelling the fumes seeping down on the wind. They did not shout or cry out but sighed in spontaneous unison as the first thread-worm of fire wriggled over the top of the far slope and at once explored downwards, dragging behind it an ever-widening tail.

Jethro Carter watched the creeping lava. He saw it as a serpent, a messenger of its master Satan, challenging him to do battle. His hands were wet with the sweat of anticipation as he clasped them together and gave thanks. O God, receive my thanks for this chance to fight the good fight and lead this heathen people finally into your sacred house. O Lord, preserve my strength and courage and go with me into this struggle to overcome the dark forces of evil and cleanse this place of ignorance and iniquity. O God, receive my thanks . . .

Ruth knew that her brother was mad. She had known for a long time, since not long after she came to the valley. She had told herself she was wrong, that she could not understand what it was that drove a good man like Jethro, that she was casting him in the role of madman to cover up all her own guilt and inadequacy. But as the months passed and became a year, then almost two years, she had faced the truth and found that a new gentleness grew in place of the hero worship she had lavished on him all through her life. As she stood on the hillside with the heat of the fire on her face, her nostrils flaring at the acrid stench of the lava, she knew that the life she had known was coming to an end. That was sad but she was not sad. She was excited. She was excited at the thought of being truly free at last, free of family, free of friends, free of the place she was born in, free, free, free. It would be like being born again. That was funny. Rebirth at twenty-five. Maybe not so funny. Maybe that was when a woman should be reborn. Maybe that was when a woman could really start to be a woman. Ruth was excited and she felt guilty about that. She knew that no one should be excited at the prospect of a man committing ritual suicide.

The Carters were an ordinary American family. They were not wealthy but they certainly were not poor. They lived in a small town surrounded on three sides by rich farmland. On the other side were the mountains. Mr Carter sold life insurance. He sold a lot of it because he was known and liked and trusted. The folks in the town would tell you he wasn't really a salesman at all; more like an adviser, a friend. His company rated him a good salesman. The Carters were decent people. They had a fine home in a street of fine homes carefully spaced on both sides of the tree-lined street, each home with a garden back and front and no fences anywhere. They did all the things that decent people do. They were involved in the community, they went to church every Sunday, they saved and invested, they were proud of their children. The Carters had reason to be proud. Jethro was a fine boy. They were disappointed when there were no more children so they were thrilled when Ruth came along when Jethro was fifteen and well through high school. He was pleased too even though all the kids at school made cracks about it.

It was a good town to grow up in. In the summer there was the tennis club and swimming in the river and barbecues and hayrides and dances and the country fair and the Fourth of July. In the fall there was Thanksgiving then skating and snowballing and skiing and sleigh rides and Christmas. It was like a lot of small American towns. It was not washed by the tides of violence and discontent. There was no colour problem. There were no ghettoes. There were no protest marches. The occasional reefer smuggled back from a visit to the city was a much discussed secret. The boys still got their kicks from throwing their hotrods around the country roads and groping on dark porches after dances.

When Ruth was five her big brother appeared in a uniform and there was a lot of laughing and handshaking and photo taking. Mrs Carter cried and said how proud she was. Jethro told Ruth that he was now a soldier and was going away to fight bad men called communists in a place called Korea. She was eight when he came back. He was the same big brother but he was different. He was thin and his uniform seemed too big for him. He looked old like a man not a big brother. The bad communists had put him in prison and been cruel to him but he had discovered God which was funny because he had always gone to church and must have known about God. It was not the kind of thing you forgot like brushing your teeth. His eyes were different too, bright, shining, like that picture of Jesus in the Bible book. Maybe that's what discovering God meant, making your eyes bright and shining like in the picture. She would practise that in the mirror in her room every night. She could never get it right and that made her sad. But she was not sad when Jethro began not to be thin any more. Mrs Carter spent a lot of time in the kitchen and there was so much food all the time that Ruth who knew about diets from her mother's magazines started to worry about getting fat. They were a happy family again. Then Jethro went away to college to learn to be a proper disciple of the Lord and Ruth didn't think she'd like him dressed in these long robes and with a beard. But that was all right because when she went with her mother and father to see him graduate he wasn't a disciple at all, just a reverend with that back-to-front collar like the reverend at the church back home. Ruth was almost eleven. After that she only saw Jethro at long intervals. He was a missionary in the Pacific islands. She was a teenager and increasingly sceptical about almost everything but she loved getting his letters. They helped her get super grades in English and Geography for she could write with huge authority on Polynesians and Melanesians and coconut palms and coral islands and even headhunters. She realised that Mr and Mrs Carter were just a little bit disappointed in their son. Mrs Carter was given to saying things like: 'After all, he seems to be happy doing what he's doing and that's something, I suppose.' Mr Carter handled it in his usual jocular way. 'One thing about Jeth's job, he'll never be short of pulpit fodder, not with all the blacks there are in the world.' It was time for Ruth to go to college.

It was her first real experience of the world outside her hometown. She had blossomed intellectually in her last year at high school so college with its limitless frontiers of knowledge was exciting. She wanted to study everything. She did almost that in her freshman year. Books, lectures, earnest discussion; she buried herself in them all. She tried a few skirmishes with the social life on campus but found it irrelevant. Most of the boys seemed to be all hands and most of the girls spent a lot of valuable learning time comparing their tallies. Ruth attracted boys because even then she was good looking, still on the plump side, just beginning to lose her inheritance from Mrs Carter's home cooking, but already showing signs of her later statuesque beauty. It was her brain that quickly scared boys off. Egghead women start with a big handicap. She was not worried. She found her heroes among the faculty members. Ruth was a sucker for older men. Max Haltone was older, almost as old as Jethro. His speciality was Ancient American Civilisations. She took his course in her senior year. To Max, Ruth was a dream come true; a beautiful woman with a brain and an enthusiasm for his subject. They dated off the campus. It was against the college rules but what did rules matter when a unique blending of minds was possible. Ruth was exasperated. There seemed to be only two kinds of men in her world, the ones with hands and the ones with heads. She had hoped she might meet a physical man with a brain. Maybe marriage was the answer. Yes, that was it. Max was an old-fashioned man. They got engaged the day she graduated. Her parents were delighted. Mrs Carter told all her friends that Ruth was engaged to a non-medical doctor who was also a professor. Max went off to

27

excavate a new site in Peru. Ruth stayed home and thought it over, decided she was too young for marriage, sent back his ring and flew to Europe.

This was living. Swinging London, bottom-pinching Rome, beer-swilling Munich, Left Bank Paris. Peoples and places with centuries of tradition yet revolutionary zeal for all the great new human crusades. In Paris she met Harry. He was English and a true anarchist. He was hairy and hippie. He was a spellbinder. He decided that Ruth was his kind of woman. The love thing was out, that was decadent, but of course they'd have sex. He knew it all. She was a bit surprised at what a careful planner he was. She had to go on the pill. She went on the pill. It said on the packet that she was protected from the first swallow. Harry knew better. They would wait a month. They waited but Ruth would wait no longer. Harry had certainly been around. He had very practised hands. But he couldn't contain himself. Ruth was left hanging in an excruciating limbo. He did not even try to hand her down. For the first time in her life she swore at another human being. She cursed him with a desperate fluency which would not have disgraced a trollop. He wept. She patted him and comforted him then went and tried to soak herself clean in a hot bath. Next day she had her hair done, bought new clothes, burned her jeans and men's shirts and sandals, and flew back to the States.

The States and home, then back to college for a post-graduate course and Max. Even before that all started up again Ruth knew it would never work. She felt trapped and turned for help to her big brother. She had not seen him for six years. He wrote back and told her of the great new work God had called him to. He had been led, the first white man ever, to convert a strange and primitive people who lived in a secret valley high on a great mountain. She must go there and help him. To Ruth it sounded like Shangri-La and the Garden of Eden in one and the same place. So

Max Haltone got his ring back for the second time and the Carters said brave, puzzled good-byes and Ruth came to the valley of the Pochaks.

She had come fired with Jethro's enthusiasm and stayed because she loved and respected the Pochaks. It had been a great adventure for her, from the long trek through the jungle, up the mountain, along the cliff paths where there seemed to be no paths, and through the maze of caves till suddenly the whole valley was spread out beneath her. Jethro had been there to meet her and she had her first pang of disappointment. She wanted to see the valley, meet the people, see where they lived, discover what they grew and ate, what their customs were and listen to their folklore. Her brother only wanted to show her his church. It was on the floor of the valley, half-way along its length. It was in white painted clapboard with a single bell tower like a pic-ture postcard American country church. It was almost finished. He walked her down to it and the little house beside it, telling her with pride of how he had got the Pochaks to cut and haul the timber, to build the church and furnish it, to mix the pigments to make the paint, to fashion the bell. This was his way of leading his pagans to the true God. The Pochaks had no writing so Jethro had turned their language into a phonetic script and had translated the Bible. Soon he would be ready to start his crusade and Ruth was there to help him. It was all part of a divinely inspired plan. To Ruth it was as if he had wasted all his effort. Even in these first moments she knew he felt nothing for this ancient people. He was obsessed with their conversion and his own fulfilment. She saw Jethro's church as an obscene transplant in that uniquely primitive place.

Ruth learned the language quickly and was welcomed into the Pochak community. They saw that the woman stranger was not like her brother. She wanted to learn, not to teach. She listened as they explained the wall paintings

29

and sculptures in the caves, she marvelled at their way with stone, noting that the built arch was a feature they took for granted. She watched the women making their pots and the men forging metal tools and weapons. She worked with them in their tiny plots terraced into the sides of the valley. She tried to understand their complicated social structure. She counted the men and women and children and saw why polygamy was the rule. She listened to their folklore and found herself remembering Max Haltone and his theories of westward migrations across the Pacific from South America. The Pochaks were pale skinned, a sort of yellowish brown; their long heads with prominent noses and slightly slanting eyes might have come from the same stock as the South American tribes; their knowledge of the arch reminded her of the Chimus of Peru who had that knowledge long before the Incas who conquered them. She did not have the expertise to relate their language to that of other peoples. And she found it impossible even to guess at dates for the events recounted in their folklore. The Pochaks had no sense of time. A day was a passage of the sun from east to west. A night was the darkness when the sun slept. Childhood was when a girl could not conceive and a boy could not do a man's work. A lifetime stretched from birth to death. Anything that had happened before the birth of a living member of the tribe was in the past. It might have been a hundred years or a thousand years. For all their sophistication in building and husbandry, the Pochaks knew nothing of counting past the numbers of their fingers. Death was as unremarkable to them as birth. Death was the end of life and the Pochaks saw it as the same end of the life cycle that they saw in their crops and their pigs. Death was not a cause for joy or grief. It was just to be accepted as a fact. Dead bodies were not preserved or buried. Land was precious. The dead were burned, the bones pounded, and the remains raked back into the soil. Ashes to ashes and dust to dust. There was no ancestor worship, no complicated deities. There was only the mountain their mother and the sun their father, and the wise man and the chiefs who saw the signs and heard the gods' voices and told the people what they saw and heard.

Ruth found herself trying to bridge a growing gulf between her brother and the Pochaks. She listened to both sides. Jethro told her how he had been working at a jungle mission station with the pygmy headhunters when a group of pale men from the high valley had come to barter. Jethro had felt a great surge of power and it was plain that the pale men were dazzled by the power showing in his eyes and pleaded with him to come back to tell their people the good news. Manutami, the wise one, told it differently. His son, Pagotak, the chief, had gone to barter and had seen on Jethro the long awaited sign from the sun their father. He showed Ruth the sign which Jethro had given him. It was her brother's fraternity ring from college, a thick gold band set with a red stone. The tears of the sun and the sun itself. Jethro told his sister of how he had been led to the spot on which to build his church and how he had inspired the Pochaks to help him build it then come to worship in it. Manutami explained that it was the way of the people to make a house for any stranger but since no stranger ever stayed long in the valley they always chose a place on the rocky base of the valley and not on the fertile slopes. Of course they all visited the stranger when he asked them. That was their duty as hosts. Ruth asked the old man if there had been many strangers. None during his life, except when the yellow men came in war. Then a white man came and taught the young men to fire guns and carried with him a big box that spoke to his chiefs far away. But they did not build him a house; he stayed in the caves so that the yellow men in their flying birds would not see him and make holes in the ground with their magic. The Pochaks remembered

31

that white man. He came and went and did them no harm. When the flying birds came he taught them to lie still in their caves till the birds went away. He told them that the birds could not land in the valley because the mountain their mother made winds to keep her people safe. Some of the young men went with this white man to fight the yellow men beyond the valley.

It was Jethro's crusade that finally separated him from the Pochaks. Ruth tried to reason with him but it was no use. He wanted the children's nakedness covered. He wanted the women's breasts hidden. He railed against polygamy and promised awful punishment for those who did not forsake their worship of the mountain and the sun. He wanted to baptise children, and have Christian marriages, and bury the dead and revere them with monuments. He wanted to stop the body painting and tattooing and the initiation rites. He claimed to be the only source of truth. His church stood empty and the people asked Manutami for a sign. It would come, he told them. Ruth too believed it would come. She wondered if she was in some way bewitched by these pagans. She was shocked to realise that she had turned against her brother. She wondered if it was her presence that had somehow launched him on his mad crusade. In the night he would rise and toll the church bell to rouse the whole valley. She would find him on his knees in the church praying for the power to perform a miracle and win his heathens for the Lord. Jethro's deterioration took many months. In her distress, Ruth wrote to Max. She did not tell him about her brother. She told him about the valley and the Pochaks. She needed someone to talk to. Mail was slow. It had to wait till some of the men were going out of the valley to trade. She had forgotten about the letter when Max's reply arrived. His excitement was infectious. He had been thrilled by her letter. He asked a host of questions. He felt she had found the last piece in a jigsaw that had puzzled him for years. He was putting together an expedition. Ruth's enthusiasm evaporated in a cloud of dismay. What had she done? The Pochaks had welcomed her and she had betrayed them to the inquisitive world outside. Max would come with his expedition and his enthusiasm and a wealth of the best intentions and begin the destruction of this ancient people. She tore up the letters and prayed that something would stop Max. She was not sure if she prayed to her own god or to the mountain and the sun.

One day the mountain spoke and Manutami said that soon the man stranger would be put to the test. Jethro said that the Lord had spoken to him in the night and told him that he would be the instrument in a miracle for the greater glory of God. The mountain shook and holes opened in its sides and the lava poured out and down and all the people of the valley gathered to watch the test. The lava was halfway down the opposite slope, running, stopping, spreading, running again, aimed all the time at the little white church.

Manutami stepped forward and lifted Jethro's left hand. Ruth saw the glint of gold as he put the ring back on his finger. 'It is the time, my son.'

Jethro started down the slope. He said nothing. He did not even look back at his sister. His eyes were fixed on his church and the flowing lava.

Ruth watched him all the way down to the valley floor and across and into his church, the white painted timber showing pink in the red glow from the sky. She felt oddly separate, as if she was not involved, as if everything she saw was just a moving picture on a screen. The lava ran and reached the bottom of the valley. It hesitated, searched left and right, gathered strength and poured on towards the shallow ditch round the mound on which the church was built. The tongue of fire split and laid a moat of molten rock round the church and the little house. The moat filled and the lava crept up the mound. The paint blistered and the blisters burst and tiny puffs of smoke spurted then drifted upwards. The lava reached up over the mound and touched the walls and suddenly the church was on fire. It seemed to burn interminably, the shape unchanged as if contemptuous of the flames. Then the whole building collapsed in a shower of sparks and the flames roared high into the air and the bell tolled crazily as its tower toppled and fell into the furnace. Amen.

Manutami spoke to her. 'He died well, my child. Like a man fighting for his home.'

Ruth nodded. 'I too am a stranger. I must leave the valley.' She was dry eyed. She felt no pain. She had lost her big brother a long time ago. If Jethro was right he was already in that kinder world he had been seeking ever since that camp in Korea. Ruth felt like a traitor. She wanted to tell the old man about Max. She wanted to warn him. She had had another letter, asking if she was all right, wondering why there had been no news. There had been delays with his plans but everything was set. He gave her dates. He would now be on the island. But she said nothing. The Pochaks seemed well able to take care of strangers.

Manutami was speaking. 'When the sun returns, the men will lead you back to your people.'

'No.' It was out before she knew what she was saying. But it was true so she went on. 'I don't want to return to the mission station. You must take me somewhere else, far away, the other side of the island, where I'm not known.' Her eyes pleaded with him. 'I died down there with my brother. Now I must start again, a new life.'

The old man watched her. Pagotak, the chief, spoke to him. He nodded. 'We understand. There is a man of your people whom we trust. He came to us when the yellow men came in war. He is a man who understands. You will tell him we sent you and he will take you where you want to go.

The drums of the river people and the jungle people say he is not far away.'

She nodded. Anything. Anyone. Anywhere. Just not back to the mission station and that world. Anywhere but this place she loved and hated. She looked once more at the glowing wreckage of the church and the house. Good. Everything she owned had been destroyed by the flames. Now she could start anew.

Chapter 3

Smith waited till the sun was well up, throwing its light directly on the water at the foot of the cliff. The clear sky was marred only to the north and west by the drifting smoke from the burning forest. He had climbed the hill before dawn and seen that the lava flow had stopped. The sky then was reflecting the patchwork of fires growing wherever there were trees and growth to feed on, being stopped by the bare gullies that scarred the mountainside, changing direction with the fickle winds. So it had been just a lava flow after all. An overture without an opera. Last night he had wondered if the lava was only the prelude to some cataclysm that would tear the mountain apart, opening up the ground, collapsing cliffs, raining death from the sky. That had just been a bad dream. There was nothing to worry about. Now he could get on with what he came to do.

He watched the light on the water. It was time to go. He checked the rope coiled carefully on deck and tied one end round his waist. He stepped down the ladder and grimaced as the water touched him. It felt cold after the hot sun. But he was grinning as he swam across the pool towards the cliff, aiming upriver of his diving point, letting the current drift him down. He had done it so often he hardly thought about it. His mind was already beyond the dive, inside the cliff. He gripped a familiar spur of rock with one hand and looked back to check the rope. It lay in a lazy arc across the pool. He filled his lungs with air and dived. His left hand trailed down the smooth rock, his eyes probing ahead through the water. There. The entrance showed as a darker splash on the rock. Both hands gripped the rock as he let his body and legs sink level with the passage. He spun over on to his back, pushed his arms inside the passage, let his fingers find grips and pulled himself in. This was the best way to get through, face up, hands pulling along the roof of the tunnel, feet paddling. Odd. No resistance, no thrust. There was always one or the other as the river water surged to and fro through the tunnel. The top of his head took the full force of the impact. His eyes saw lights where there was darkness, air spurted from his mouth as his muscles slackened. What the hell? He steadied himself with his hands, held his breath, blinked to try and clear his head. Better. His fingers explored. There was rock all round. Ahead as well. His chest ached. He expelled some air. Try once more. Maybe it's just some rock blocking the floor of the tunnel. No. It's solid and smooth, one piece, not a lot of little pieces. It's as if the inside of the cliff's split and this bit's dropped into the passage like a portcullis. Let's get out of here.

He put his hands out and pulled himself back along the tunnel. Not so easy this way. Damn that rope, it's snagging my legs. Don't kick. Leave it be. You don't need your legs. I need air though. Hand over hand. That's it. Legs into the river. One more pull. Out. He lifted his head, kicked his snared legs and blew out as he rose. He broke surface and gulped in air, screwing up his eyes against the light. The current moved him as he filled and emptied his lungs. He untied the rope, freed his legs and let the rope drift clear. He swam upstream on his side, staring at the cliff, beginning to realise what it meant. There was no way in from the river. There was no way to finish his task.

You're a silly old fool, Smithy. Serves you right. You could've finished it last time but no, not you, you had to squeeze a few more weeks of ecstasy out of your crazy life's work. Now you can't finish it. Never. Wait a minute. If I can get up on top of the cliff, I can go in the way I did that first time. Then back out on to the top and down here. And how do you get up that cliff? It's as smooth as a Chinaman's chin. Or do you mean to walk round and up that burning mountain till you reach the top of the cliff? And even if you did, is the shaft still there? You know something's slipped inside there. Most likely the shaft's closed up. You're not much help, are you? Why should I be? There's nothing in there you really need. There's no profit in it, not the way you play it. It's just your pride that's hurt. You just can't stand being beaten. Aw, shut up.

He lay on his back and looked up at the sky, paddling with his hands to keep himself still against the current. He grinned. You're right, you know. It's a big joke anyway. This just makes it a little richer. That's more like it, Smithy. Accept the inevitable then tell yourself it's really all for the best. You've survived that way for a long time. Knowall. Have it your way but if I were you I'd be thinking about what might be slipping in all these other cliffs down through the gorges. And I'd be getting me and that boat to hell out of here and down the river. All right, point taken.

He rolled over and swam for *Mermaid*. He grabbed the ladder and looked back across the pool. Pity. He ran a hand over his hair and felt the lump where his head had struck. Well, I didn't dream that. That's real enough. He climbed aboard.

As he straightened up on deck he saw the woman. Her mouth was open as if she was going to call out. He saw the pig at the same time.

'Keep quiet.' He didn't shout the words, just spoke them very clearly. These wild pigs could be nasty. They weighed in at better than two hundredweights, moved fast and had mouths as mean as their tempers. 'Don't move. Keep quite still and don't make a sound.' He stepped slowly sideways along the deck, his eyes fixed on the pig's head peering out from the undergrowth. It was moving to and fro, casting about for confirmation of the scent. The pigs had bad eyes but keen noses. The light airs round the pool had saved the woman. One strong puff of wind on to that searching nose would start the charge. Smith could see the woman on the edge of his view. She was rigid, staring at him, still open mouthed. He reached the wheelhouse and stretched a hand in through the open window for a rifle. He found it and lifted it through and slipped off the safety catch. It always had a bullet in the chamber. 'You're all right now. I have you covered. Just walk slowly forward and get on board.' The pig's head had disappeared but he could see the undergrowth moving. 'No, not towards me. Just straight across from where you are. That's it.' He watched till she climbed the rail and stood on deck. Only then did he put on the safety catch, reach the rifle back into its rack, and turn to look at her.

She was good looking, very good looking. He blinked his eyes and felt the lump on his head. This is quite a day. She wore denim slacks tucked into jungle boots, and a bush jacket. There were thorn tears here and there and she was spotted and streaked with black soot. He walked across the deck.

'Sorry about that reception but these pigs are a bit hostile sometimes.'

'Pigs?' Her voice was cracked from a dry mouth.

Smith pointed. 'There he goes.'

Ruth saw the movement in the undergrowth. 'Oh.'

'Pity I didn't get a shot in. I like a bit of roast pork.' She looked even better close up. 'Now where the devil did you pop up from?'

'From the mountain. I came down . . .'

'Wait a minute. You're dry. I'll get you some water.' He fetched the pottery jug that hung in the wheelhouse. 'Here you are. Oh damn, I suppose you need a glass or something.'

'No, this will be fine.' She tipped the jug and drank. Then she poured some water into her cupped hand and splashed it over her face. 'That's better. Thanks.'

'You were saying you came down from the mountain.'

'Yes, the Pochaks brought me. They stayed in the forest. They wouldn't come this far. It's part of their forbidden land, you know.'

'I know. How do you know?'

'I know all about the Pochaks. I've been with them for almost two years.'

'Missionary,' said Smith.

'You make it sound like a cussword.'

'Sorry about that.'

'That's OK. I know what you mean. But I'm not a missionary. My brother was.'

'Was?'

'Yes. He . . . he died last night. Some lava came into the valley. He'd built a church, you know. An American church, in the valley. The lava burned it down.'

'He was inside?'

She nodded.

'Why didn't someone tell him? Lava doesn't flow that fast.'

'It's a long story. You wouldn't understand. He wanted it that way.' She looked up at him. 'Maybe you would understand. He was . . . he was going to make a miracle.'

Smith raised an eyebrow. 'Act of God, eh.' Then he frowned. 'I'm sorry. That was in very bad taste.'

Ruth stared at him. 'No need to apologise.' She smiled. 'You do understand. The Pochaks said you'd understand.' She giggled. 'Act of God.' She laughed. 'Act of God.' Her whole body shook with laughter. 'Act of God,' she shrieked hysterically. Then the tears welled up in her eyes and she gasped for breath and stumbled against him and wept like a child.

Smith put his arms round her. 'Let it go,' he said quietly 'Let it go, whoever you are.' Her hair was in his face. He could smell it, sooty from the mountain fires but female. His hands felt the warmth and movement of her sobbing body. It was quite a day. He felt the heat of the sun on the back of his neck. Quite a day and not yet noon.

Ruth did let herself go. She felt no shame at weeping on this stranger's shoulder. It seemed easy and natural, even comfortable after the night before and that morning. So much had happened, the scene had changed so often that already Jethro's death seemed far in the past. She had tried to sleep but her brain was a jumble of doubts and regrets and feelings of guilt fighting a losing battle against the prospect of new freedom. It seemed to be a physical thing, as if new life was pulsing through her body. Then the quick tropic dawn and her last look at the valley and out through the secret ways to the smoke and flames of the burning mountain. It had been a long walk down. Then that formal touching of hands, palm to palm, when Pagotak and his men left her, a dignified little ceremony but somehow comic there in the jungle. Her lone walk the last few hundred yards and her first sight of the boat. It had seemed quite unreal after the mountain. A ship in the middle of the jungle, a ship like no ship she had ever seen before, clean and bright in the sunlight, its jutting prow with its magnificent mermaid in flight, fleeing that phallic funnel glistening near the stern. Her memory threw up a picture of a little girl in a sun bonnet at a country fair, speechless at the beauty of a tasselled and ribboned stallion. Then the man had risen dripping from the river on the other side of the boat and his voice froze her with fear and calmed her and brought her to safety. It was like coming home. There were no more tears. She watched the last of them running off the brown skin of the man's shoulder to disappear into the mat of hair on his chest.

She raised her head and his hands slackened on her back. 'Thanks. I'm fine now.' Her fingers wiped at her eyes. 'I must look an awful fright.'

'You look fine,' Smith told her. 'Come on. Let's get off the deck.' He led the way to his den between the wheelhouse and the saloon and switched on the fans.

Ruth flopped down on one of the settees and let the fanned air play on her face. 'Bliss.'

He stood in the doorway and watched. 'Have you got a name?'

She sat up and nodded. 'I'm Ruth Carter. And you must be Captain Smith.'

'I'm Smith. I don't know about the Captain.'

'This is your ship, isn't it? Doesn't that make you the captain?'

'Maybe.' It was funny how small things warmed you to people. She'd said 'ship' not 'boat'. 'But then I'm engineer, bosun, deckhand, and cook as well.'

Ruth shook her head. 'It seems too big for just one man.'

'I try to be big enough. I like being on my own.'

'Oh.'

'What does that mean?'

'Pagotak said you'd take me down the river.'

'Did he now? And how is Pogostick? Haven't seen him for years.'

'Pogostick? Is that what you call him?' She smiled. 'That seems very undignified for one of the chiefs of the Pochaks.'

'So he's a chief now, is he? Serves him right.'

She tried to puzzle that out. 'He sent you a message. He said to tell you he hoped you'd now feel his debt was paid.'

Smith laughed. 'Cheeky bugger.'

'Pardon.'

His voice had a hard edge. 'Listen to me, Ruth Carter. If

you're going down the river with me, don't expect me to apologise every time I swear. I swear quite a lot.'

'I'm sorry. It wasn't that. I wondered what kind of debt it was that was so funny.'

'Maybe I'll tell you when we get to the sea. If we get to the sea.'

'If?'

'There's always ifs when Mama Mountain's playing games. Come.' He went through into the saloon and pointed to the stairway. 'Since you're the only passenger, you'd better have the best stateroom. Down there. Help yourself to anything you need.'

'Thank you.' She hesitated. There was so much more she wanted to say but it seemed unnecessary. It was as if this strange man knew all about her and understood. 'Thank you,' she said again and went down the steps to the big cabin.

Smith went back to the wheelhouse and opened the magazine locker. Damn Pogostick. Damn Ruth Carter. This might be a rough enough trip without a mixed-up virgin in search of her private paradise. He checked the gear. There was enough for four depth bombs if he needed them. Empty paint drums with tight lids and holes punched all round. Stick dynamite. Plastic explosive. Time pencils. Stones in little bags. Sticky tape. He shut the locker and looked across at the cliff. It seemed as solid as it had ever been. Maybe I'm worrying about nothing. Maybe the passage through the gorges will be clear. So then there's nothing to worry about. But if you do strike trouble, you're ready.

He stood and listened, a small smile at his mouth. There was water running in the pipes to the big bathroom. How d'you feel now, Ruth Carter? Now you've seen that bed and bidet, or are you the kind who calls it a footbath? D'you still want to go down the river with safe Captain

Old-enough-to-be-your-father Smith? He chuckled and pressed the starters. The engines whined and burst into life. He tried the wheel hard over both ways. He went aft and let go, then for'ard and started the windlass and took in the head rope. *Mermaid* swung away from the bank and started pulling up to her anchor. He watched the cliff coming close. Good-bye cliff. I won't be back. I don't know why but I know I won't. He watched the first shackle coming in over the windlass, walked aft and set the engines to dead slow to stem the current, back up to the bow to see the anchor clear and housed.

Going down through the gorges Smith always took the con from the monkey island above the wheelhouse. He climbed up and faced aft, the wheel at his back, the engine controls close to hand. He closed the throttles and let the current move *Mermaid* astern to the channel out of the pool. She gathered way quickly. He put the engines ahead to slow her then reset them to swing the stern a few degrees to correct her into the gap between the rocks. The stern slid through and he checked the bow over his shoulder. His hands flew from throttles to wheel, back to throttles, port, starboard, slow, half, full, ahead, astern, stop. It was a virtuoso performance but there was no written score, always improvisation on a theme of survival, notes, phrases and timing dictated by the constant variation of current, depth, ground, wind and weather. The boat curved clear out of the gap into broader water and the cliff was lost to view. The audience of parrots squawked their approval and the monkeys raced along the branches chattering their frenzied applause. Smith bowed and smiled to his gallery. He felt that lightness and joy he only got when *Mermaid* was free on the water and the con stretched him to the limit.

The boat was dropping down to the bend into the first gorge. It was an easy channel, wide and gradual. He took her through and round with only two engine movements.

There was the spot where the boy Blik had hauled him out of the river. Dear Blik. We're going to clash soon, you and me. How do I know that? I don't but I feel it in my bones. Everything seems to be coming to an end. Maybe it's my age. Maybe I'm as far round the bend as people've thought I was for years. Then maybe I'm not.

'Where are you, Captain Smith?'

Ruth's voice startled him. He had forgotten about his passenger. 'Up here,' he called. He turned as she came up the ladder, then turned back quickly to check his course. My God, she's not good looking, she's a raving beauty. That one glance had painted an indelible picture on his mind. Her hair was loose and long, bronze. She was wearing a pair of trousers, the legs rolled up tight on her shins, and one of his shirts tucked and tied at the waist to make it fit. The breeze sculpted her breasts in the silk. Uncanny. He blinked and looked again. No doubt about it. She could have been the model. But she probably wasn't born then. And there was no model. I carved that mermaid out of my head. She was standing beside him and his nostrils flared as they caught the scent of the toilet water. Correction. Maybe everything's not coming to an end after all.

'Are you feeling better now?'

'Like a new woman. You certainly look after your passengers, Captain.'

'My friends call me Smithy.'

'And your passengers?'

'They've been known to leave me without a name.'

She laughed. 'Why are we going backwards? We are going backwards, aren't we?'

'We're going stern first if that's what you mean.'

'Sorry.'

'It's the only way I can control her in fast water as narrow as this.' He moved the throttles to check the drifting stern.

'It's scarey. Like in a canal with high sides.'

He nodded. 'Good fun though.' The end of the gorge was coming up. 'Could you hand me the binoculars from that box? Thanks.' He put them up and scanned the water ahead. It looked clear. He looped them round his neck. 'I don't know about you but I'm peckish. Would you like to rustle up some sandwiches?'

'OK. Where's the kitchen?'

He grimaced. 'The galley's at the after end of the saloon.' He shook his head. 'Down, inside, and keep going thataway.' He pointed.

'You'll make a sailor of me yet, Smithy. D'you make all your passengers work?'

'There are worse fates, Miss Carter.'

She started down the ladder. 'Than death, d'you mean?'

She was out of sight by the time he turned. I like you, Ruth Carter, but I'm damned if I know how you can look like that figurehead's twin. Maybe I'm just imagining it. Must have a look when we anchor.

He was steering *Mermaid* into the second gorge when she came back with a plate of monster sandwiches. 'I see I'll have to make a cook out of you too. Didn't your mother teach you that food's got to look good to taste good?'

'Please yourself. I'm hungry enough to eat the plate.'

'It's a good looking plate.' He ducked as she raised her hand. 'Truce.' He opened his mouth and stuck his head forward. She held out a sandwich and he took a huge bite. He chewed and swallowed. 'Not bad.' She held out the rest of the sandwich. Smith's eyes were on the side of the gorge. He slammed both throttles to full ahead and the exhaust roared at the funnel top. Ruth's head came up in surprise at the noise and she lost her balance as the boat stopped in the water. She went down on one knee and the plate crashed to the deck.

She was angry. 'That wasn't funny, Captain.'

'That's not funny either,' Smith told her. He was point‍ing at the sheer rock wall. An open crack zigzagged up all the way to the top. He swept it slowly with the glasses. Chips of rock ran in little rivers down the gash. He closed the throttles and the boat drifted downstream again.

Ruth felt his anxiety. 'Is that bad?'

'It's not good.' He glanced down at her. 'If you're going to stay on your knees you might like to try a prayer.'

She got up then bent and collected the food from the deck. 'What do I do with this now?'

'Eat it of course. I keep a spotless ship.'

She put a sandwich together from the bits and held it out to him.

He took a mouthful and ate as his eyes roved along the wall of the gorge and down to the narrows at the end. 'See. I'm still alive.'

Ruth pretended to ignore him and bit into her own sand‍wich. She found her eyes following his along the cliff and across the water. Nothing seemed amiss but she already knew that this man didn't joke about anything that might mean danger to his ship.

Smith had the boat slowed right down. If things were happening to the gorge walls, things might also be happen‍ing to the river bed. If he was going to hit rock underwater he wanted minimum impact. The other way was to turn *Mermaid*'s bow downstream and run at full speed to clear the danger area. That was not his way. There was no sign yet of immediate hazard. At full speed the stern would squat down into the water and increase the draught. And if he hit a rock spur at full speed he could rip the bottom out of her. Easy does it. Tortoise beats hare.

The narrows were clear and he coaxed the boat expertly round the bend into the last gorge. His eyes at once searched along the cliffs on both sides. They looked re‍assuringly solid. He checked his watch. It had been a good

47

run. 'Another half-hour should see us through.'

'Thank goodness.' The relief sounded in her voice. 'I'm starting to feel a bit hemmed in. Oh, look at that.'

He checked her pointing finger. The bird was standing on the far bank puffing and smoothing and stretching its gorgeous plumage. 'Bird of Paradise. Haven't you ever seen one before?'

She shook her head.

'That's how the river got its name. Don't usually see them this far up. That's a good sign. They're quick to sense trouble.'

'She's magnificent, Smithy.'

'He.'

'Oh.'

'It's only man who lets his females outdo him. And then only so-called civilised man.'

'Whose fault's that?' she asked.

He turned his head and looked at her for a second or two. 'I'm not complaining.'

It was a new experience for Ruth. She had been mentally stripped by a lot of men but never like that. Smith's stripping was frank and complete but tender and appreciative. Desire without lust. It was as if she was a piece of sculpture, studied, understood, coveted; something to be felt with loving hands and experienced with mind and body but protected from depredation. She felt wonderfully clean. Her heart raced. She watched the river till she was sure of her voice. 'Beautiful bird, beautiful place.'

'You'll change your tune, my girl, when we're through into the slow water. There's a hundred miles of malarial swamp to the sea.' He paused. 'Were you on malaria pills up on the mountain?'

'No. There isn't any malaria up there.'

'There is where we're going.' He nodded astern. 'I'll give you a bottle as soon as we're anchored.'

'You're the doctor, Captain.'

With no more signs of movement in the rock Smith let *Mermaid* pick up speed. He made it all look deceptively easy. Graceful too, thought Ruth, the way his arms, hands and fingers move in harmony like a harpist plucking a melody from obedient strings.

'Almost there,' he announced.

She could see the end of the cliffs and the broad sweep of water beyond, water that was smooth, oily brown, almost sinister after the clear running water they were in but a welcome change from the stark, bright, noisy prison of the gorges. She longed to be through the narrows, free of the menace of the sheer rock walls, drifting aimlessly on the quiet water with its lush jungle greenery stretching away as far as the eye could see; but she longed too to preserve the moment, to thrill to the feel of the boat rushing down the river, to watch Smith's fingers composing their wonderful, primitive symphony.

There was hardly any warning, just a brief rumbling that juddered up through the boat. Ruth turned to Smith in alarm. The characteristic half smile had gone from his mouth. His hands were still but his eyes scanned the cliffs in constant search. He knew that rumbling was a warning quivering through the river bedrock. The boat had not hit anything. It was receiving and transmitting the tremors through the water. There was less than half a mile to run to safety. It might yet be all right. He felt rather than saw Ruth beside him, tensed like a bowstring. 'Don't worry,' he said quietly. 'Don't worry.'

It happened so quickly that even his eyes were left behind. He heard the single crack like a giant whiplash, saw the cliff on the north bank open up as if pierced from within, was lost by the speed of the spreading wound, saw only the huge overhang severed and slipping down. His hands opened both throttles without his willing them and the boat slowed and stopped, stemming the current. The vast slab of rock slipped silently then hit a buttress and burst with a roar into a thousand boulders which cascaded down into the narrows. They thundered to the ground at the base of the cliff, piled up, bounced, spread and spilled over like a waterfall of stone into the channel. The quiet water beyond disappeared behind a pall of dust. Smith heard Ruth's long frightened sigh as the noise of the falling rock died.

'That's a bit awkward,' he said. Ruth seemed transfixed by the puffing cloud of dust. 'I said that that's a bit awkward,' he repeated distinctly.

She turned. There was no fear in her eyes, just shock. 'Yes, I heard you.'

'D'you know what we do now?'

'No.'

'We make a way through.'

The shock gave way to puzzlement.

'Down below.' He pointed. 'Down the ladder to the wheelhouse.' He watched till her head disappeared, speeded the engines to give the boat some headway, and ran for the ladder. He went down with his hands sliding on the rails, his feet never touching the rungs. In the wheelhouse he closed the throttles and let the boat slip back downriver.

'Where are we going?' demanded Ruth.

'We're going to look.'

He held *Mermaid* in the water fifty yards above the narrows. The dust was settling. The water was still running through the channel but it was broken water, not just fierce with the compression of the banks but tumbled, jagged, broken as it fought its way over and round the dam of fallen rocks. He took Ruth's arm and pulled her across behind the wheel. 'Can you steer?'

She looked up in astonishment. 'Of course not. I don't know anything about ships.'

'You're going to learn, Ruth Carter.' He put her hands on the spokes of the wheel and gunned the engines to drive the boat back upriver. He slowed them to hold her steady at the first broad stretch. 'It's quite easy. Don't look at the wheel. Look right ahead. Pick a mark. That spur of rock with the bush will do. See it? Good. All you do is keep the bow pointing at that bush. Now, if the bow falls off to port—no—if the bow starts to move to the left, you bring it back on to the bush by turning the wheel to the right. If it moves to the right, turn the wheel to the left. Don't worry. I'll be around.' He took his hands off hers. She was too tense but he said nothing. He leaned over and opened the magazine locker and lifted out two of the drums. The bow was falling off to port. Her reactions were too slow. He could see her muscles tightening. She spun the wheel hard to starboard. The bow checked and came back. Her muscles slackened. The bow kept coming, past the marker, gathering speed. Her hands were frozen to the wheel. He stretched round her and whirled the wheel back to midships and then on to port. The swinging bow checked then crept back. Midships. On target. 'Little and often,' he told her. 'As soon as that bow moves, correct with the wheel. Not too much. Just a couple of spokes. As soon as she starts coming back, bring the wheel back to midships.' She nodded. 'It's midships when this turks head's at twelve o'clock, in front of your tummy.' He lifted one of her hands and pressed her fingers round the cord braiding on the top spoke.

'I see.' She sounded breathless.

'Don't worry. You're doing fine. You're a born sailor.' Her stiff shoulders slackened and a tiny smile caught the corner of her mouth. He started making up his bombs.

'What are you doing?' she asked.

'Curing our spot of bother.' He glanced up at the bow. She's good. She's doing fine. He held up what looked like a piece of Plasticine and moulded it in his hand. 'Take some plastic explosive, surround it with sticks of dynamite.' He zipped round two strips of sticky tape to hold the lethal collection together. 'Pop that in a waterproof bag. Take one timed detonator and insert in plastic. Put bag in old paint drum full of holes. Weight drum with bags of stones.' He looked round. Her eyes were fixed on the bow but were wide with disbelief. 'Don't worry. I know what I'm doing.' He looked aft and judged the distance. 'I set the time pencil, seal the bag, snap the lid on the drum and drop it over the stern. Current carries drum down towards channel. Water fills drum through holes. If I've judged it right, drum sinks just as it reaches the channel and lies on the bottom against these fallen rocks. Bang and, with any luck, we've got a way through.'

'I hope you're right.' She stole a glance at the drums but looked away at once. She was scared even of firecrackers.

Smith made up a second charge and juggled times in his head. Less than half a minute to float down to the rocks. Allow half a minute to seal up the drum, carry it aft and drop it. Want to be sure they sink properly. Say a minute and a half all told. He set the first pencil to a minute and three quarters, sealed it and slammed on the lid. Next pencil, one and a half minutes, seal, close. 'Hold her just as she is, Ruth.' He ran out and along to the stern and heaved the drums overboard. Back in the wheelhouse he adjusted the engines and watched the drifting drums. They were more than half-way there already. He checked his watch. Half a minute. He smiled as he saw them settling down in the water as they filled through the holes. They were in the rough water. One was caught on an obstruction. The other drifted on. Sink, you bugger, sink. It hesitated, stopped, sank. The first one was out of sight too. A minute and a quarter. His tongue flicked along his lips. Five, four, three, two, one. Come on, come on. The first explosion came as a kick through the water to the hull, then the water in the channel bulged upwards and broke with a muffled roar. He grinned as he saw rock in the air. A second kick and a second explosion. He looked round at the bow. 'Good girl. You're doing fine.' The water in the channel was smoothing. He put the glasses up and took stock. 'Damn, damn, damn.'

'What's wrong?'

'There's something still there, right in the middle.' He took out the other two drums and started putting the charges together. He looked aft to check the distance again. His eyes went up the north cliff. Nothing new there. Then he saw the crack in the cliff on the other side. God's truth, not that too. Nothing was falling. He made his decision. 'I'll take her.' He took the wheel and opened up the engines.

'What's the matter? I thought I was doing fine.'

'So you were. I'm just going to turn her in that big pool up there.' He was taking an awful chance. Once *Mermaid* was turned, he was committed. Even full astern would barely stop her in the water. There would be no chance of turning and running upstream again. It was once and for all. It was a chance all right but if that south wall came down there wouldn't be enough explosive on the island to get them out. He steered into the pool and spun the wheel hard over to port. Starboard engine full ahead, port full astern. The bow swooped to port. He played the throttles to keep her stern clear of the bank. The bank ahead was covered by the swinging bow. It looked as if she must hit. But there was room. The bow was caught now in the current, the south cliff soaring aft. Midships the wheel. They were round. There was no going back. Smith checked her into the middle of the stream and put both engines astern to slow her. He lifted the first charge. 'Ruth, as soon as I set this and close the lid, you take it out and drop it over the side.'

She shook her head. 'No, I can't. I'm scared of these things.'

He grabbed her and turned her face to his. 'You're more scared of me, girlie.' He let her go. 'And when you drop them, lean well out to make sure they don't catch on a fender.' He revved the engines to full astern. The boat was almost unmanageable bow first in the current. One and a half minutes. He set the pencil, sealed the bag and closed the lid. 'Off with you.'

She took the handle, ran the few steps to the side, leaned out and dropped the drum. She lay across the rail trying to calm herself.

'Hurry it up,' he shouted. 'Here's another one.'

She ran in, lifted it, ran out and dropped it.

Smith watched the drums drawing ahead of the boat, swinging like pendulums in the water, steadying as they filled and started to sink. He eased the throttles and *Mermaid* chased them downstream. Thirty seconds. Ruth was back in the wheelhouse, leaning, panting, and staring at him fiercely. 'Thanks,' he said. 'You did well.' He glanced at her. 'You won't hate me so much when we're through to the other side.'

She was oblivious to the ship, the river, the cliffs, the danger. There was just Smith. If she had had the strength in her legs she would have stepped over and hit him. She hated him not just for making her lift the bombs. It was the way he had done it and now the way he read her face like an open book.

One minute. The drums were sunk and the upturn of the bow was starting to cover the channel. Smith ran his eyes up the south cliff. The crack seemed no wider. Seventy seconds. He gunned the engines astern again to slow the drift. 'Wake up, Miss Carter, and hold on tight.' Eighty seconds. The bow had shut out the channel. Come on, come on, blow before you blow my bloody bow off. Ninety seconds. He felt the kick and had the engines ahead before the water rose and roared and shut off vision. A harder kick. God, that's close. The water seemed to erupt right under the bow, spurting up through the hawse pipes, rising in a huge wave, hanging there, deafening the ears with its bellow, crashing down on to the bow as the boat rammed into it. sweeping aft along the deck throwing its cargo of splintered rock in all directions. The wave broke against the wheelhouse, threw itself through the open windows, split and rushed aft along both sides of the deckhouse, swirled, gurgled and slipped off back into the river.

Smith had ducked as the water poured in over him. He was erect again, shaking his eyes free of it, feeling the check in the boat's way, knowing there were still rocks down there. Go on, you beauty, push them, roll them, fight them. He felt every grinding shudder as if his own body was taking the beating. Go on, you beauty. Suddenly no pain. His feet and hands sensed the free thrust of the stern and the scything cut of the prow. They were through to the quiet water.

Noise faded astern. The noise of the racing river caught and amplified by the cliffs, the noise of crashing rocks, the noise of the depth bombs and the following noise of exploding water, the noise of the boat fighting to stay alive. Now all sounds were small, delicate. The soft splash and chuckle of smooth water caressing the hull, the muffled rhythm of unstrained engines, the soughing of still air teased and tumbled by the moving ship, the tick-tock of wood drying in the scorching heat of the afternoon sun.

Ruth leaned in the side doorway letting all her terror drain away, renewing herself in the warm breaths of air and the blissful quiet. 'We made it,' she whispered to herself. 'We made it and it is like Paradise.'

'They don't call me Paradise Smith for nothing.'

She looked round, startled. He was erect behind the wheel, his face in profile, eyes searching ahead, fingers closed round the spokes. He was like a proud beast guarding its territory. 'You're quite a man, Smithy.'

He turned his head. 'And you're quite a woman, Ruth Carter.' Her drenched shirt was a transparent second skin. Quite a woman. He spun the wheel hard over to round *Mermaid* to her anchorage.

He hung over the bow watching the anchor chain tighten then sag as the boat was brought up. He recalled his promise to himself and stretched farther out to view the figurehead. He frowned. The right breast had been neatly amputated by a rock splinter fired up by the last bomb. Have to call her *Amazon* now, I suppose. His eyes moved up to the face and head, back down the long sweep of bronze hair. The resemblance was quite uncanny. Balls. It's just my imagination. But when he turned away he saw the same face and hair, farther away but unmistakable, framed in the wheelhouse window. He walked slowly back along the deck, kicking idly at the residue of stones from the narrows, wondering about that figurehead he had carved a quarter of a century before.

He joined Ruth at the window and they looked back up at the mountain. The black smoke from the burning forest was thinning and dispersing.

'I wonder how the Pochaks are,' she said.

'They'll be all right. They're good survivors too.'

'Hmm. I wonder what Max will think when he finds I'm not there.'

'Max?'

'Max Haltone.'

'Should I know him?'

'No. He's a professor.'

'Why shouldn't I know a professor?'

'I didn't mean that. He's a professor at my old college back home.'

'What's a professor doing visiting an old pupil out here?

More than a professor maybe.'

'A friend. Just a friend. I was engaged to him once. Twice.'

'Make up your mind.'

She puzzled at that for a bit. 'I mean I was once engaged to him twice.'

'I suppose that's a bit better.'

'You know what I mean.'

He nodded and promised himself that he'd hose away all the stones and mud when the sun went down and the heat retreated. 'So why's he here?'

'To study the Pochaks. Didn't I say that?'

'No. They don't like strangers up there.'

'I know.' She remembered Jethro and was quiet for a few moments. 'I feel bad about that. Sort of guilty. They were very kind to me.'

'Is that why you ran away?'

'That and other things too.'

Smith felt he already knew enough to write her life story. 'So you told your professor about the Pochaks. Why's he so interested?'

'He thinks they're the key to a theory he has about some of the old tribes of Peru migrating across the Pacific. That's his subject, Ancient American Civilisations. I wrote him all about their folklore, the way they build in stone with proper arches, about the white men who are supposed to have come long ago to try and convert them, about their forbidden ground, about the valley. I told him everything. I was a bit down. I needed to communicate with someone. I know it was wrong of me.'

'Stop worrying,' Smith told her but he was more alert than his casual voice suggested. 'He'll maybe never reach the valley. It's not a place anyone's ever reached unless the Pochaks wanted them to.'

'You don't know Max. He'll get there. He's a very determined man is Max if he's after something. Especially if it's been dead and buried for a few centuries.' She paused. 'He'll get there. He's very thorough. He doesn't fly off on wild goose chases. He travels with personal introductions from his friends in Washington.'

'To the Pochaks?' laughed Smith.

'No, to the President.'

He took time to digest that. 'President Blik?'

'That's right.'

Dear Blik. I was right. It's all starting to happen. He stared up at the mountain but he saw only a flurry of pictures. Japs, clifftop, shaft, falling body, drowning body, threatening body, half-caste boy. There were several more reels. The smile on his face was thin, joy and achievement diluted with a vision of death.

He stood up straight. Routine. There was still the daily routine. It's been quite a day, Smithy. Quite a day and still not even sunset.

Chapter 4

President Blik was bored. He needed some excitement. He had been at his desk in Government House for the past month. There had been no excuse to travel. Blik was an inveterate traveller, a jet-set statesman. He enjoyed the quick change of scene, the thrust and parry of the diplomatic round. He was a man who needed tension to tone him up. Travel gave him that tension and also relieved it in a constant cycle. It was like his other passion, hunting. The thrill of tracking, the surge of pleasure and anticipation when the prey was cornered, the excitement of the kill, the awful anticlimax with the dead beast at your feet, then the ritual of gutting and skinning, the male heartiness of the campfire and the rising tide of expectation for tomorrow.

For interviewers Blik had a well polished, heart-rending explanation of his frenetic activity. Like all the best lies it had strong veins of truth but was heavily edited and embellished. It all stemmed from his childhood (that always went down well), an orphan of the war, abandoned to survive as best he could in the jungle, hunted by the Japanese, showing even then his talent for leadership, rallying the jungle tribes who usually fought and ate each other, teaching them to fight and eat the Japs, winning the war only to find the colonial masters returning to recover the lands they had stolen long ago. Escape and the struggle for the education needed to free his people, scholarships to the States and on to Paris. Then back to rouse the tribes and march in triumph to fling the Dutch into the sea. As the writer who did the recent *Time* cover story said, 'It's pure Grimm by way of Kipling and Edgar Rice Burroughs.' But he didn't write that.

There were still old planters sipping their Bols in Amsterdam who blamed not Blik but Paradise Smith for their exile back to their homeland. And there were government men in The Hague and London who congratulated themselves on the way they had used Smith and Blik to preserve the British part of the island while the Dutch cut their last link with the East, leaving behind an impoverished little independent republic and thus at last giving themselves the satisfaction of kicking the Indonesians in the crutch.

If the president bent the truth in his propaganda he was always strictly honest with himself. He never forgot his debt to Smith. Not just all the education he had paid for but the feeling of having roots. The fun of long holidays on the boat between school terms, the formal dinners in the saloon, just the two of them, the jokes, and the talk and the planning for a brave new world. And even when Blik left the island for university, the link of long letters and the certainty of coming home. The encouragement to plan for when the island was not a colony, the help in starting the revolt, the disagreements, reconciliation and on to victory. Then the shock of discovering that Smith had rigged the whole thing with the Dutch and the British.

It was then that Blik had promised to kill Smith if he ever caught him out again. Eight years ago, eight long years of each hearing of the other but never meeting. There would be no meeting now. Blik was playing on another stage. He could not afford to acknowledge a past that made a mockery of the past he had invented but he had long since admitted to himself that Smith had been right to do things the way he did. There would never be cause now for Blik to redeem his dreadful pledge. Smith was a man to be trusted. The president was repaying his debt by walking his political tightrope according to the rules Smith had taught him.

He pushed the papers aside and got to his feet. Schemes,

schemes, schemes. Suddenly everyone wanted to sell him something. Correction. Everyone wanted to give him something. For the first seven years of the republic he had had to scrape along as best he could with occasional scraps dropped from the rich countries' tables. Even when he made the capital a free port there had been little interest. But now, with the Americans finding their presence unwelcome in Japan and Okinawa and the Philippines and somebody in Washington remembering a story told him by a blue-eyed half-caste about a superb natural harbour in the Western Pacific, Blik's republic had been discovered.

To hear them tell it, governments and companies were really philanthropists. Power and politics were unimportant spin-offs from their big hearts. Of course it was a game. The rules required a player to tell lies all the time, knowing that the other player knew they were lies. When the move passed to the other player, his first lie was his acceptance of the first player's lie then he added a whopper of his own. The object of the game was to reach an agreed solution without ever admitting one's true motives. Played on the political level the name of the game was diplomacy. There were several variants in commerce; the investment game, the development game, there had even been the exploitation of resources game but that had been dropped as inappropriate in an ex-colonial territory. There was a crude version known as the what's-in-it-for-you game but the president refused to play that one. Even the most delicately wrapped package failed to tempt him. That was one part of his debt to Smith. He had no use for personal wealth. Greedy people were vulnerable. Anyway his position gave him all he needed and he had no intention of retiring.

He walked over to the window and stared down on the town and the great sweep of the harbour, almost locked in by the long island offshore. That was the key. An American base on the island, alongside the new international airport.

The free port to attract the greedy tourists, made greedier by their tax burden back home. Lots of night life down in the town. Exotic tourist attractions; camera safaris hunting birds of paradise, pig hunting expeditions (the brochures would call them wild boar) with genuine headhunters as escorts, shark fishing offshore, crocodile shooting in the estuary on the far side of the island. There was no need to let the mining companies tear up the tribal lands in their search for minerals, no need for hydro-electric schemes or heavy industry, no need for the expensive education of the jungle people who had no use or desire for it. Blik's tight-rope was anchored between the selective development of the harbour and the capital, and the preservation of the primitive interior. Just the week before he had been bombarded with praise from a planeload of conservationists applauding his stand as an example to the developed world. Prosperity through preservation. That's what the man said. Blik grinned. He felt better. Tomorrow I'll go out and hunt me a wild pig.

'Excuse me, sir.' It was his secretary.

'What is it, Soong?' Soong was Chinese. He had lived all his life in the capital but Blik never thought of him as an islander. Chinamen were somehow always Chinamen. He was an excellent secretary, protective, efficient, with an encyclopaedic memory. He had worked loyally for the Dutch, he was completely loyal to Blik, and would be just as loyal to any successor. Masters came and went.

'Professor Haltone is here, sir.'

'Who?'

'Professor Haltone, sir. An American gentleman. I have kept him waiting for two days but he has a letter of introduction from Mr Meister of the State Department so I thought you would want to see him.' He laid an envelope on the desk.

'What does he want?' asked Blik, walking over and picking up the letter. 'What's he a professor of?'

Soong shrugged. 'I'm afraid I don't know, sir.'

Blik slit open the letter and shook out the folds. 'Hmm. I suppose I'd better see him. Ted Meister's a good friend.' He looked up. 'Send him in, Soong.'

'Thank you, sir.'

The president tidied his papers and sat down at his desk. He lifted a paper at random, placed it on the blotter and stared at it with furrowed brow to complete the picture of the harassed head of state.

'Professor Haltone, sir.'

'Mr President Blik, sir.' The American was tall and well built. He strode across the room with a boyish eagerness which pushed his head forward and stooped his shoulders. His hand was outstretched. 'It's truly very good of you to see me.'

Muscular Christian, decided Blik. He half rose and shook hands briefly, retrieving his own before it was crushed in the giant grip. 'I'm just sorry you had to wait, Professor, but the day just doesn't seem to have enough hours for me.' Soong had a chair ready and Blik motioned the American into it. 'And how is Ted?'

'Pardon, sir?'

'Ted. Ted Meister. How is he?'

'Oh, he's well, I think. Just fine.'

'Good. And his charming wife? And these three delightful children?'

'Well, I suppose they're fine too. I don't really know them.'

'What a pity. Lovely people.' Blik picked up the letter and read it again. 'Ted says here that you're a historian, anthropologist and archaeologist, Professor. You seem to be a very busy man.'

Haltone smiled shyly. 'I'm really a historian, Ancient American Civilisations. That led on to my other two interests.'

'And how can I help you? We're rather a long way from Ancient America here.'

'That's just it, Mr President, I don't think you are.' Haltone sat forward in his chair. 'I've had a theory for some long time now that about a thousand years ago some of the peoples of Peru migrated westwards across the Pacific.'

'I thought that had already been proved. Wasn't there a Scandinavian fellow who floated across on a raft?'

'That was Heyerdahl. Norwegian actually. He certainly proved that migration was possible. I believe I can now prove that it really happened.'

'And my little country has a place in your theory?'

'It sure has.' Max pulled his chair closer. 'I believe that about 900 AD some of the Chimu people started on just such a migration. The Chimus were a very cultivated people who were later conquered by the Incas. But before the Inca wars, the Chimus had their own wars and it was after one of these that this migration started. I think of them as The Lost Tribe of the Chimus.'

'What a picturesque title for a book.'

'Indeed yes and, of course, Mr President, I will be writing a book if this all works out.'

'Go on, Professor.'

'Well, I have a very good friend here on your island. A Miss Carter, Miss Ruth Carter. She used to be a student of mine. A very able young woman. She wrote and told me about this Pochak tribe and I realised at once that she'd found what I'd been looking for.'

'You mean that the Pochaks are your Lost Tribe.'

'I think so maybe. You see, sir, that letter made me realise that I'd been sitting on a mine of evidence for years and had never known it was evidence.'

'Tell me, Professor, who is this Miss Carter? How did she come to know about the Pochaks?'

'She's been staying with them for a year or two. Her brother's a missionary, Jethro Carter. He's built a church in this valley where they live.'

'Is that so?' Blik pulled over a pad and made some notes. 'And you want to go and visit the Pochak valley, is that right?'

'Correct. I believe I need permission.'

'Yes, you do. You see, Professor Haltone, the Pochaks do not welcome strangers. The terrain is such that no one can reach the valley without the Pochaks agreeing to welcome them. Of course, there are a few of us they trust, the few who have actually been there.'

'You have been there, Mr President?'

'Yes, a long time ago.' He could see that Haltone was almost out of his seat. 'During the war. I was on the run from the Japanese. I was a bit shot about. They took care of me, hid me, nursed me back to health. Fine people. Primitives have much to teach us, Professor.'

'Indeed yes, sir. That's something I often tell to my students. Well, if you know them, and with Ruth there, they're certain to agree to my trip, don't you think?'

'Possibly. But I'd have to know more of your evidence before making a decision. So far it's just a vague theory.'

'I've got it all here, Mr President.' He opened his case and lifted out a box file. 'It's all here, sir, all indexed and annotated.'

Blik lifted the file and winced at its weight. He slid it to one side of the desk. 'Thank you. I'll read it all with interest.'

'Can I call back in the morning?'

'Professor, I do have a country to run and occasionally I like to spoil myself with a little sleep.'

'Of course, sir. It's just that I'm keen to get started.'

'Don't you find the capital's night life amusing? We should all relax now and again.'

'No offence, Mr President, but it's not really my scene.'

'You surprise me. I'd have thought that Orange Street was full of interest for an anthropologist.' He tried to picture Haltone in the red light district.

Max flushed. 'I guess I prefer my evidence dug up from the ground.'

'How interesting.' The end of Blik's nose was itching. Now that's even more interesting. He scratched it slowly. Why should my hunting instinct suddenly tell me that I'm going to catch a scent? He glanced at the clock on the mantelshelf. 'It might help to speed things up, Professor, if you could quickly give me a digest of your evidence.' He patted the big file gingerly.

'I can tell you about it now, if you could spare the time.'

'That's what I meant.'

'Great. Now, let me see. Where should I begin?'

'Maybe at the beginning?'

'Yes, yes, of course.' He sat back in his chair then hitched himself forward till he was perched precariously on the edge. 'Well, I suppose it started, though I didn't know it then, in London England about six years ago. I was over there on vacation and I saw a notice in *The Times* newspaper about a sale by auction in a country house. There were some things listed from Mexico and South America which I thought our college collection should have. So I cabled the States and they told me to go ahead and authorised a figure I could bid up to. I went down the day before and, sure enough, there were some truly nice pieces. The catalogue explained about this family. The family had been founded way back near the end of the sixteenth century by a man who had been in the English navy under Sir Francis Drake. He wasn't a captain or anything, he was a chief gunner. But he apparently was a very good gunner and got big prize money and probably a lot of loot on the side. He had saved his prize money and bought some land. By the time he died he was a real country squire and had laid the foundation of the family fortune. But that fortune wasn't in too good shape a few years back so the house was being sold up.'

Blik's nose had stopped itching. 'We do seem to be rather far from home, Professor.'

'Yes, sir, I know but please bear with me.'

The president nodded.

'On the day of the sale I got all the items I wanted and had them shipped back to the States. They were there when I got back home and the first thing I looked at was a rather fancy Mexican casket. It was a type I knew so it didn't take me long to find the trick and open it. Inside was a book. It fitted the inside of the casket exactly which I took to explain why no one had realised it was openable. Anyone picking it up would think it was solid and just a rather nice but useless piece of fancy furniture. The book was a hand-written journal in Spanish. The ink was very faded so I sent it round to our manuscript man and he came up with a transcription. Are you still with me, sir?'

'Just.'

Haltone hurried on. 'The journal was by a Spaniard, Fernando Murillo, a doctor and apothecary. We checked and discovered that just such a man had been killed during Drake's raid on Cartagena de las Indias in 1572, that's the Cartagena in what's now Colombia, the Cartagena that was called the Heroic City after the Spanish siege of 1815. So we can assume that the casket was looted by Drake's gunner who became the English squire.' Haltone took a deep breath. 'The journal is a record of voyages Murillo made as a ship's surgeon in his younger days and much of it is a medical record of the illnesses he treated on board ship. The voyage that concerns us is the expedition of 1525 under the command of Garcia Jofre de Loaisa who had seven ships and was supposed to follow up the discoveries of Magellan. Of course Loaisa died crossing the Pacific and only one ship survived to reach the Moluccas. But that was the ship Murillo, the doctor, was on. Now, sir, I must remind you that Magellan was killed in the Philippines in 1521 and there were then only two of his original ships left, the *Victoria* and the *Trinidad*. They eventually did reach the Moluccas and loaded with spices for the return journey. The *Victoria* reached Spain via the Cape of Good Hope in 1522, the first circumnavigation. The *Trinidad* sailed eastwards across the Pacific and disappeared without trace. Without trace, that is, until Murillo's ship picked up a demented man from a native canoe near the Moluccas. Here's an interesting problem. Murillo's journal records at some length this survivor's story but there is no trace anywhere of this story, or even the fact that the man was picked up, ever being officially recorded. We have to assume that, as we'll see, Murillo was so convinced the man's story was just a madman's ravings that he didn't bother to record any of the facts elsewhere. Also, being the only surviving ship of the fleet, everyone was pretty busy just trying to stay alive. I know this may all sound irrelevant, Mr President, but we are getting to the meat of the story.'

'Do go on, Professor. I'm fascinated.' He was fascinated more by the American's torrent of words than by the facts.

'The demented survivor claimed to be a Diego Lopez, a seaman from the *Trinidad*. Murillo knew that the *Trinidad* had disappeared almost five years previously and, from the fact that the man was found in a native canoe of very crude construction, assumed that Lopez had been cast up on some island, had survived somehow or, more likely, been held captive by natives and eventually escaped in a stolen craft. The doctor's journal suggests that, for his time, he had advanced ideas of the working of the human mind under stress. As we'll see, these ideas had developed when he was learning his profession attending victims of the Inquisition. His mistake was to start with a theory and make the facts fit it. It's not uncommon. I must admit that I've been guilty of it too. If I had read that journal more carefully and not accepted Murillo's reading of the man's story, I might have been here seeking your help several years ago.'

'You're going to say that Lopez had been wrecked on this island. Is that right?'

'That is so, sir, but it would be better if I tell it my way. If you don't mind.'

Blik shrugged. He remembered from his own university days the hopelessness of arguing with academics in spate.

'Murillo's idea was that, in stress conditions, men invented situations and experiences as a way of escape from the stress. In extreme cases this could lead to madness. He saw Lopez as a classic case because he had decided that Lopez had been living either as a captive or as a solitary survivor for all these years therefore all his crazy stories were just compensations to escape from the terrors of reality. All the details Lopez gave of this place where he had been checked apparently exactly with places he admitted to having been on previous voyages to South America and with the popular legends about the riches to be had there. The doctor's theory was that men could be shocked from madness back to sanity. Of course he didn't have the techniques of electric shock or drugs. He used red hot tongs applied all over the body. He hoped to return the man to sanity and thus discover the real truth about the fate of the *Trinidad* and what had happened to Lopez since. The tongs didn't change Lopez's story and, mercifully, he died the next day. Murillo records in his journal that he thought it a disappointing case.' Max, now thoroughly launched on his lecture, sat back in his chair and crossed his legs. 'As I've said, I took only a passing interest in Murillo's journal. Remember that this was just one case in a long list of cases he recorded. I passed it, the journal, on to a colleague of mine who was researching a book on the great voyages of discovery. He went on to Europe to get closer to the original sources and I forgot all about Murillo and Lopez. Till Ruth's, that is Miss Carter's, letter. That letter had enough information to make me sure that I'd found my Lost Tribe of the Chimus. But some of the details struck a chord in the back of my head. It was a couple of days before I traced that chord and remembered Murillo's journal. That was an exciting piece of research, Mr President.'

'I'm sure it was but I can't see why it was necessary. Miss Carter's information was, you say, enough. Why bother about this Murillo journal?'

'That's a very good point, sir. Firstly, the Lopez story provided confirmation by eye witness of what is only folklore passed down by the Pochaks. Interesting point there, by the way, is that the last known chief of the lost tribe in Peru was called Poquaque. But I was explaining the importance of the research. Much of the importance to me was in analysing why Murillo got it wrong and, for that matter, why I missed the point at my first reading. Just think, sir, that if the Lopez story had been reported and believed the whole emphasis of exploration and conquest might have been shifted from South America west across the Pacific. Remember that this was 1525, one year after Pizarro's first voyage down the coast of Peru, a voyage that was a conspicuous failure. If Pizarro had been told Lopez's story he might have sailed westwards and never attempted his later invasion of the Inca empire. The whole course of history might have been changed.'

'There seems to be a great number of ifs in that theory, Professor.'

'Of course, but what a fascinating speculation.'

Blik's nose was itching again. 'What was there in the

Lopez story that might have attracted a man like Pizarro?'

'The promise of El Dorado, of course.'

Blik's nose stopped itching but his nostrils widened. 'El Dorado. The city of gold.' He decided that Haltone was shrewder than he looked. He had spun the story out, keeping the what's-in-it-for-you gambit till now.

'Well, yes, that's what it came to mean. The words actually mean The Golden Man, supposed to be a native king who appeared covered in gold dust on special festivals but even that seems to have been apocryphal. But certainly El Dorado came to mean a place where gold was to be had in abundance.'

'And where on my island is it to be had in abundance?'

The professor shook his head. 'As you probably know, Mr President, treasure stories are notoriously misleading and always grossly exaggerated. In this case the treasure isn't gold, it's the solution of the disappearance of my Lost Tribe.'

'Of course. But you didn't finish the Lopez story.'

'Ah yes. Well, Lopez claimed that the *Trinidad* had run into storm after storm on her way eastwards and was eventually wrecked at the mouth of a river full of sand-banks and infested with crocodiles. The survivors, about ten of them, made their way up this river towards a huge mountain like the mountains back home in Spain, with snow peaks. On the mountain they found this people like the Indian peoples of South America. They converted them to Christianity and got from them vast quantities of gold. This gold came from a great lake half-way up the mountain. Lopez said they stayed there for several years but then the natives rebelled. All the Spaniards were killed except Lopez who escaped and, after a pretty rough trip through jungles and swamps, found a canoe and sailed out to sea. I can see you're away ahead of me, sir.'

Blik had got up and was staring at the relief map of the

island which stretched along one wall. 'Go on, Professor.'

'Where Murillo, the doctor, went wrong was in starting by believing that all this was just the ravings of a madman and then trying to explain it. For instance, he knew of no large land mass in that part of the Pacific. Remember that it was not till the next year, 1526, that Menezes discovered New Guinea and, because your island lies between the two equatorial currents, it was another two hundred years before anyone put it on the map. So Murillo decided that, with no land mass, there could be no river so Lopez's river was imagined or remembered. The doctor asked Lopez about the Orinoco, which had mudbanks and a wide estuary and was infested with crocodiles, and Lopez agreed he had been there. On the big mountain Murillo had two explanations. High mountains and lakes of gold appeared in almost every story of El Dorado, and since Lopez compared the mountain with the Spanish mountains, this proved that his story was a blend of hearsay and homesickness. And so on. The doctor managed to explain the whole Lopez story as a mad illusion. He was born too soon. He'd have made a great psychiatrist.'

The president smiled at this uncharacteristic lapse into humour. Or was it academic bitchiness? 'So you think that the Pochaks were the people the *Trinidad*'s survivors met, converted, and were in the end killed by.'

'That's so, sir. And Ruth's information confirms it all and supplies even more detail.'

'But no details of where our El Dorado is?'

'Not really. It's certainly not the lake. I checked a report the Dutch did in the 1930's. They found alluvial traces but nothing more than that. If it's anywhere it'll be where these Spanish corpses are. The story goes that the Pochaks put the dead Spaniards with the gold they loved so much and abandoned the place for ever. They call it the forbidden land. From what I've read about that mountain, sir, with all its eruptions and changes of shape, I sure wouldn't like trying to find that place after four hundred and fifty years.'

'No, I see that.' Blik was suddenly formal and brusque. 'It's been fascinating, Professor. You must excuse me now.' He pressed the buzzer on his desk. 'I think I'll be able to help you later on. Not immediately I'm sorry to say because, as you probably know, the mountain has been spilling lava again and the seismic reports suggest continued instability. We couldn't risk anything when we've promised Ted Meister to look after you, could we. Ah, Soong, the professor's leaving now.' Blik silenced protest with a handshake. 'Keep in touch with Mr Soong. He'll know when it's safe for your journey.'

The president walked slowly back to the map. With his finger he slowly traced a path up the river and through the gorges to the head of the river. It was a trip he had done many times. It was a dangerous trip and, as a teenager, he had often asked Smith why he took all these chances just to cut down some trees. He always treasured the answer he got. 'The trees aren't important, Blik. It's the challenge of beating the gorges. The marvellous quiet up here at the cliff. And because this is where we met and we're special.'

Soong was back. 'Is there anything you need before I go, sir?'

'Yes. Yes, there is. Tell Major Loder I'll need the helicopter in the morning.' The major was seconded as an aide from the planning team over on the American base site.

'Yes, sir. Good night, sir.'

Blik remembered. Greedy people are vulnerable. Pigs are greedy. Trust is all that matters between two people. He drove his fist into the map, bursting through the papier mâché and the wire form, taking out the mountain and the lake and the gorges. Tomorrow I'm going to hunt me a greedy, vulnerable, untrustworthy pig.

Chapter 5

Ruth dabbed her mouth with the napkin and sat back in her chair. 'That really was a marvellous meal, Smithy. Where in all the world did you learn to cook like that? Is this how you always feed your passengers? Can I afford it? You haven't told me what this trip will cost.' She stretched then relaxed. 'I've probably done permanent damage to my figure but I'm not worried. Is that because you served whisky with it?'

Smith got up, tidied away some of the plates, lifted over the coffee percolator and lit the spirit lamp under it. 'Will I answer your questions all at once or one at a time?'

'Please yourself. I don't suppose it matters what the answers are. I wouldn't be asking them if I was in a restaurant. I'm just grateful for a wonderful meal.'

He nodded. They both watched the flame under the coffee and listened to the sounds of the glass and the water heating, the soft cycling of the big overhead fan, the whirr and buzz of the moths and insects clustered on the mesh screens in the window openings, fighting to reach the lights inside.

The meal had been cleverly balanced. First a jellied consommé built on a chicken stock with a subtle blending of local spices. Then on to what Smith called the Paradise Platter, a traditional Indonesian *rijstaffel* with extra dishes culled from the best of Indian and Chinese cookery. It was not so much a main course as a continuing experience from bland to sweet to sour to fiery, back to bland, some flavours delicate, some mysterious, some violent. It was a study in the limitless potential of blending at the table. He had let her experiment, then he had made suggestions and watched with growing pleasure as she became more and more adventurous. She had asked for water but he had given her a malt Scotch, well iced and diluted, explaining that this was the British Raj's only contribution to the Indian table but an important one, cooling the palate but giving a slowly dilating warmth to the stomach, a much better solution to the problem of what to drink with Eastern food than the Dutch answer of ice cold lager. As a sweet, a cold *compote* of island fruits dressed with Grand Marnier.

They had talked through the meal only about Ruth. Smith was an old hand at finding out about people. Her answers to his questions had confirmed his first impressions but it was the way she ate and drank, the enthusiasm with which she followed his suggestions about the food, her obvious joy in being where she was, doing what she was doing, that filled in his picture of her. She was escaping from but she was also escaping to. He understood what that meant. Resilience and optimism were basic to Smith but he liked having her at his table to remind him of these qualities and blunt his premonition of disaster and death.

Ruth broke the silence. 'I can understand why you go to all this trouble when you have a passenger. It's an occasion, isn't it? Like a party. An excuse to do something special.'

'I'm sorry to disappoint you but I eat like this every evening in port or at anchor.'

'When you're on your own?'

'Yes.'

'But why? All this bother and no one to appreciate it.'

'Not no one. I'm always here.'

'You know what I mean.'

'Yes, I know what you mean. You mean that people belong in groups. You mean that being alone is only good in small doses to make you realise what a joy being with other people is. It's a popular point of view. And since it's unavoidable in organised society, it's claimed to be natural. My view is exactly the opposite. Being alone is what life's about for me. Being with other people only makes me value being alone. And it reminds me that, even in groups, we are all really alone all the time. You look surprised, Ruth. Think about it. Haven't you ever walked into a room full of people and felt alone? Of course you have. You stand on the fringe and watch all these puppets talking and drinking and laughing. If you're like most people you don't enjoy that. You feel alone but you don't like the feeling because you think you're missing something. Then you spot someone you know and they greet you and suddenly you belong and the world changes from sombre black and white to glorious Technicolor. All you've done is find a crutch to rest on. And the others have found a new crutch for themselves in you. You feel you're giving by talking, laughing, even listening. Of course you're really getting. This is a getting world. We're all getters. Even the most honest, well-meaning givers, they're getters first and foremost. Maybe you'll say you can't do one without the other. I wouldn't deny that but I believe it's important to know which is the prime mover and which the reaction. That's the first step in getting to know yourself. That's something that being alone has let me do, given me time to put myself under the microscope. Some of us have to do it because most people don't ever have the time. They're too busy being busy, doing all the essential things that society decrees are necessary for a full and happy life, the essential things which are only trivia manufactured to fill in the space between birth and death.'

'Stop, Smithy, stop. I was only trying to thank you for a lovely meal. How did I trigger off that broadside?'

Smith gave her a small smile. 'I was just trying to show

you that you didn't know what you meant when you said you did.'

'And you were using me as a crutch.'

'Touché, Miss Carter.' He watched the water rising in the percolator, waited till it burst into the upper glass with a frantic bubbling and sucking, watched it draining down as coffee. He snuffed out the spirit lamp. 'Yes, I did get diverted. I was going to explain why I eat properly in the evening when I'm on my own.'

'I know why. It's for the same reason you shave and put on a shirt. To stop yourself going native.'

He shook his head. 'Not at all. There's nothing wrong with going native as you put it, but that's another argument. The reason's quite different. It's because food's important to me. Not as a refueling operation. That's why most people eat. They take in fuel, burn it up in their body engines to make power, then get rid of the waste. It's just like my diesels. For me it's different. For me, eating is the same kind of experience as making love or winning a battle. It doesn't just satisfy, it extends and enriches. It hoists me on to a different plane, lets me see new dimensions.'

'That I understand.' Ruth patted her stomach.

Smith laughed. 'Have some coffee.' He poured two cups. 'Maybe that'll dull your wit.'

'I'm sorry, Smithy.'

'Don't apologise. I was being pompous. I deserved it.' He pushed over a dish of dark chocolate medallions. 'Help yourself. They're a Dutch habit.'

Ruth bit off a piece of chocolate and stirred sugar into her coffee. Smith got up and took a cigar from a humidor on the sideboard. He held it up. 'Do you mind?'

She shook her head.

He lit it carefully and came back to the table.

Ruth's nose wrinkled. 'Oooh. That smells rough.'

'Tastes good. Island tobacco. The old Javanese make them for themselves.'

'I know. You're going to say the women roll them on their thighs.'

'I'm not because they don't. But do get the story right. They're supposed to roll them on the insides of their thighs.'

'Is that important?'

'It seems to be to the people who tell the story.'

Ruth shook her head. 'I won't be drawn. The next thing you're going to say is that everyone who tells that story is sexually frustrated.'

'That's a safe bet.'

'Why?'

'Because everyone is, at least some of the time.'

She smiled and sipped coffee. 'You're a strange man, Smithy.' She took another chocolate and looked round the saloon. 'You're the kind who has to win all the time. You could be winning in the States or Europe but you choose to live like a hermit out here in the middle of nowhere. Why's that?'

'There are a lot of reasons.'

'And you're not telling?'

'I've got no secrets. It's a good place to live. I got accustomed to it during the war. I don't work too hard. I make a good living. I've got all the time I want to read and think. I have no commitments. I'm my own boss. I enjoy life. All that makes me a non-starter in the winning stakes back in your world.'

'There's a flaw in there somewhere,' said Ruth, 'but I'm dashed if I can spot it. Is there any more coffee?'

He poured then topped up his own cup.

She took a sip and laid down her cup. 'How did it all start, Smithy? You and *Mermaid* and the island, I mean. Or have you always been here?'

'It was me and the island first. *Mermaid* came later. It

was like everything else, just chance. You see, I'm not a captain because I own this boat. I'm qualified as one. That was my job. I was at sea. I was Second Mate of a ship that happened to be in Port Bancourt in '42 when the Japs came. They got the ship. The wreck's still in the bay. As it happened I was at that moment stoned out of my mind on a plantation up in the bush on the British side of the mountain. The invasion didn't take long. We were cut off so we faded into the jungle. That's when I got to know the tribes and the country. I wouldn't have lasted a week without them. As it was I lasted over three years till it was all over.'

'So that's when you learned to like being alone.'

'That's it.'

'But after the war, why didn't you go home? Where is your home anyway?'

'I suppose I'm still British but I didn't have a home to go back to. I wanted to do a bit of living and Port Bancourt was quite a wild town in these days. Then I found *Mermaid*. It was love at first sight. She was in a helluva state but I knew I wanted her. I didn't even have enough money to have her hauled out of the water so I started trading in war surplus.' He laughed and spun his chair so that he faced her. 'Ruth, you only need one day in that game to know for sure the world's mad. It was the right time of course. The island was piled high with stores. Then came the bomb and the end of the war. For my first deal I took an option on a godown stuffed to the roof and sold it all for cash to an Australian the same day. That gave me money to pay off the option and a bankroll to buy more. In a few weeks I had enough money to start refitting *Mermaid* and still leave quite a bit in the bank. So I stopped trading and started work on the boat. I suppose that proves I'm not your kind of winner after all. Two of the men I dealt with then are now very respectable millionaires.'

'Maybe it proves you are a kind of winner.'

'That's as may be but what it certainly proved was that I was then already tired of being back in the world. All I wanted was to get the boat ready and get away.' He stubbed out his cigar. 'End of story. I've been getting away ever since.'

'How long's that?'

'Twenty-five, twenty-six years.'

'That's funny,' she said with a wry smile. 'All my life.'

'I'd never thought of it that way. I suppose it has been a lifetime. A young lifetime.' He remembered guessing that as her age when he looked at the figurehead in the afternoon. He looked at her now. She's got brown eyes, not green eyes. I wonder how much more I imagined. You're getting old, Smithy. You're starting to see what you want to see.

'That sums you up, Smithy. A young lifetime, you say. Everything about you is young. You're fitter than most young men. More confident. More optimistic. More adventurous. You're one of those rare people who'll always be young.'

He held back from telling her she had missed his meaning. 'I don't know about me, young lady, but you won't always look young unless you get some sleep.' He stood up.

Ruth stretched then relaxed again in her chair. 'I suppose I should be tired but I'd like to sit here all night talking.'

'Bed,' he ordered.

She looked up at him rebelliously then smiled. 'Yes, sir, Captain.' She got up. 'Wait a minute. What about all this?' she asked, waving a hand over the table.

'Forget it. The Paradise fairies will clear it away during the night. Bed.'

'All right, all right.' She walked round the table and stopped to peer out through the screens. 'I'd like to go outside for a while. It looks lovely. The moon on the water, the mountain against the sky, the night sounds . . .'

'And the mosquitoes and the ants and the moths and the

flying foxes and all the legions of creepy crawly things . . .'

'Spoilsport.' She feigned anger as she strode to the top of the stair. Then her face softened. 'You've been very sweet, Smithy. How can I thank you?'

'By going to bed,' he told her, pointing down the stair. She laughed. 'I give up. Good night.'

'Good night, Ruth.'

In her room she kicked off her sandals and undressed. She stood looking at herself in a long mirror, turning this way and that, arching backwards, stretching up her arms till her fingers touched the deckhead, smiling all the time. She went over and sat at the dressing-table and began brushing her long hair. She felt warm inside. She brushed with long slow strokes, her eyes closed, giving herself up to the feel of the brush on her scalp then the probing of the bristles through on to her skin where her hair fell down across her body. Suddenly she shivered. It was cool in the room with the airconditioning unit working. She ran the few steps to the bed, parted the mosquito curtains and lay down, pulling the silk-covered quilt up over her. The bed and the quilt seemed ice cold. She stretched out on her back, waiting for her own warmth to warm the bed.

She had left the lights on but they were soft and restful, drawing patterns of light and shade on the deckhead. She watched the shapes. She saw her brother walking down that slope and into his church. She saw the writhing snake of lava and the church on fire. She felt no pain, no sense of loss. She saw the burning mountain and remembered her first sight of *Mermaid* and of Smith. She saw the gorges and tumbling rock, she remembered her horror of the bombs, her fear as the bow plunged into that wall of water, her relief at reaching the quiet water. She recalled their meal together. She seemed to see Smith everywhere she looked. She told herself she must be mad. She told herself he was old enough to be her father. She told herself he wasn't her father. She told herself she had been cut off from men for almost two years. She told herself she had only known him for hours. She told herself she was just the most recent of many women who had lain in that bed. She felt warm and excited, safe but sensual. She turned over on her side and pulled up her knees. She crossed her arms and hugged herself as tiredness closed her eyes and faded the pictures from her mind.

Smith watched her down the stair and heard the cabin door close. He looked over the debris of the meal and decided to leave it till the morning. He poured himself a Scotch and took it through to the wheelhouse. He leaned his back against the binnacle and sipped his drink, watching the moonlit water and the land shapes beyond. It had been a good meal in good company. It had been a long time. Longer than that, Smithy. Never. Admit it. She's special. She's special because you want her but you're not going down that stair. That's a new record. Is it your age or have you found a woman who scares you? Aw, shut up about my age. I've got bigger problems than Ruth Carter. Such as? Such as why I didn't keep on going this afternoon, why I anchored up here when I could have been down almost to the mudbanks by dark, ready to clear through to the sea at first light. That shut you up, didn't it? That's certainly a problem. Any ideas? Just one. I feel I should be running for my life but I'm finding excuses to stay here. It's as if I've run myself into a corner, as if I'm too tired to do anything but crouch there and wait. Come on, Blik, it's your move.

Chapter 6

The helicopter headed for the mountain. It flew low over the jungle, occasionally detouring to circle a village or plantation, letting those on the ground see the presidential crests on the fuselage, inviting acclamation, dispensing unseen acknowledgments. Blik was enjoying himself. He was sitting up front at the dual controls flying the big plane with a dash and expertise which kept Major Loder on a seesaw between wonder and worry. The wonder was that anyone could learn to fly a chopper so well in such a short time. In a way the major was not surprised. He had realised soon after being assigned to the president that Blik was one of these dedicated acquirers of new skills. The worry stemmed from his responsibility for Blik's safety. Loder looked over his shoulder to where Sergeant Rocco was stretched out amid the gear, singing noiselessly against the roar of the engines. Blik had said they were going pig hunting. So why all this rock climbing gear? Surely it wasn't necessary to hunt pigs up cliffs or through caves. Maybe it's just his passion for having the right clothing and equipment to hand for emergencies. Loder studied him. Like now with his baseball cap and gilt rimmed sun glasses, bush jacket with silk scarf tied at the neck, trouser legs tucked into jungle boots, tight black leather gloves on his hands. All ready for an off-the-cuff press conference. I'll bet if I took him up to heaven right now he'd sprout wings and a halo before the gates were open.

Blik's voice sounded in his head set. 'You take her now, Major. We should pick up the river in a few minutes.'

Loder thumbed his understanding and took over the controls.

Blik watched the approaching mountain, vaguely noticing the huge black scars where the lava and the fire had eaten up mile after mile of trees and vegetation, but concentrating his mind on what he would be looking for when they reached the head of the river. He had sat up late reading Haltone's notes. There could be no doubt that the place described in the demented Lopez's story was the forbidden land of the Pochaks. This woman Carter's story exactly fitted with its explanation of the abandonment of that settlement and the seeking of a safer place in the high valley. It also explained, by its detail of the later eruption that blew the whole peak off the mountain, why Lopez described the mountain as having a pointed peak. The indefatigable Haltone had included a note on this point, referring to a Dutch expedition that climbed the mountain by the west ridge in 1939 and brought back rock samples from the summit which suggested a cataclysmic eruption between three and four hundred years before. The Lopez story was vague and contradictory when it dealt with his claim to have found El Dorado but the Carter woman's recounting of the Pochak folklore was specific in placing the Spaniards' corpses and their gold store in the land the Pochaks then abandoned. It all sounded fanciful and, as Haltone had said, a hopeless search anyway in an area as geologically unstable as the mountain; unless you were the boy who once dragged a half-dead man from a river, a half-dead man who used to have nightmares about falling through the ground. A man who spent the rest of his life risking himself and his precious boat up through the gorges to that very spot.

Blik looked down at the tree tops hurtling past underneath. It seemed crazy. There were so many obvious flaws. If Smith had found treasure, what had he done with it? He would have no problems finding buyers and he was certainly astute enough to sell it where no news would ever leak out. But where was the evidence of his wealth? He would get a good price. But he was still sailing that boat of his round the coast and up the Paradise as he'd always done. Smith was not the hoarding type. If he ever did a good deal it was party time till the cash was done. They had not met since Blik became president but Blik kept himself informed. Smith was still apparently the Smith he had always known. Blik wondered about this instinct of his. Maybe he just wanted a reason to prove that Smiddy was still the same. Maybe he was getting round to eating humble pie and having Smith up to Government House and starting again where they had left off. But Blik had learned to trust his instincts. He had a scent and he was going to chase it all the way to the kill. Yes, the kill. He remembered that last meeting. He remembered his promise. 'All right, Smiddy, you say you did it for me and the country. That may turn out to be true. But you and I had an agreement, no secrets. You've broken that trust. You always taught me that everyone's entitled to one mistake. You've just had yours. If I catch you out again, ever, I'll kill you, Smiddy. I mean that. I'll kill you.'

Blik felt his mouth dry. That had been a turning point for him. Till then he had always had Smith, as father, brother, teacher, friend. Since then he had been quite alone but nagged by memories and haunted by that solemn promise. Maybe this scent would settle it once and for all.

They had been climbing steadily over the long rise of jungle to the foot of the mountain. Suddenly they were over the gorges, the river brown and green and white as it rushed between the high cliffs. Blik pointed west, upriver, and the major nodded and started to turn the plane. Blik was out of his reverie and taking notice. Something caught his eye, something flashing in the morning sunlight. He twisted round in his seat. 'Wait, Major.' He wound a hand round in a circle. 'Do a couple of wide turns. Take in that smooth water where the gorge empties.' He lost sight of it as Loder brought the plane round but then it was there, right ahead, that crazy funnel reflecting the sunlight, the white hull and the oiled woodwork making a brilliant splash on the brown water. It's like a pattern, Smiddy. You're here on your way up to do whatever it is you do; and I'm here chasing that scent. Yes, I was right to chase that scent. It's starting to happen. You're down there now, aren't you, Smiddy, watching and wondering. Well, you go on watching and wondering as I follow the river up to that favourite place of yours. There was no sign of life on *Mermaid*. 'Right, Major, that'll do. Follow the gorges.'

'Funny looking boat, Mr President.'

'You're new, Major, or you'd know that was *Mermaid*. Quite a boat and quite a skipper. Haven't you heard of Captain Smith?'

'Can't say I have.'

'You will.'

'What's he do way up here in the jungle?'

'He trades. He doesn't believe in frontiers except his own. He reckons the Paradise River is his. No one's ever taken it from him.'

'With respect, sir, who would want to?'

'That's a good question, Major.'

The plane was over the gorges again, heading upriver. Blik knew exactly where he was going and what he was looking for. He was going to the top of that black cliff at the head of the river and he was going to look for a scatter of big boulders near the edge of the cliff. It was one of the favourite stories of his boyhood when he was in the jungle with Smith, learning to speak English. It was a mystery story with thrills and a happy ending when a boy found a man who had fallen through a cliff. Later, when he had come up the river on *Mermaid* he had sometimes thought of trying to find the exact place and solve the mystery but there was no way up to the clifftop except by a long trek round and up the mountain. Smith had always said it wouldn't be worth the trouble. The result would probably be disappointing. It was good to keep some mysteries and the illusions that went with them. Blik meant to solve the mystery this time. There was no need for that long trek. The helicopter would set him down on top of the cliff.

They were over the last gorge and the spot where he and Smith had met all these years before. It was gone and the cliff was there ahead. 'That's the place, Major, that big black cliff. Get up above it and hover while I scout the ground.'

Loder nodded and edged the plane over till it hung in the air fifty feet above the plateau that ran back till it met the trees on the mountain, trees untouched by the fire which had stopped a thousand feet farther up the slope. Blik studied the ground through field glasses. It was all covered in dark green creeper. He signed with one hand and the major moved the plane along above the cliff edge to widen his view. That must be it. One small area where the flatness was broken, as if there had once been a building which had been knocked down. Maybe that was how the boulders came to be there. 'Down there, Major.' He pointed. 'That uneven bit of ground. Put her down as close as you can.'

'I can't land there, sir. I don't know what kind of ground there is under all that green stuff. I could wreck the ship.'

'I've got every confidence in you, Major. That's where I want to land.'

'I don't see any pigs, sir.'

Blik stabbed a finger downwards. Loder twisted round and signalled Rocco to put on his head set. 'Sergeant, I'm taking her down to just clear of the deck. You get out and see if there's any solid ground under all that jungle.'

Rocco got up and peered out of the open door. He shrugged. Nothing surprised him any more, especially since he had been assigned to this half-coon president.

The plane dropped slowly, the downdraught of the rotors flattening and spreading the creeper. Rocco freed the wire of the rescue winch and let about a dozen feet of it run out and dangle down outside the plane. He hand signalled the plane down till the end of the wire was in the creeper. Loder held the plane there and the sergeant went hand over hand down to the ground. He tramped the ground carefully till he was sure it was solid then signalled the plane down carefully.

'Excellent, Major,' said Blik.

'Will this take long, sir?'

'I don't know. Why?'

'Because I'm keeping the engines running and I want to watch my fuel.'

'You're very cautious, Major.'

'That's what's kept me alive so far. I don't like this place one little bit.'

'You're in charge,' said Blik, getting out of his seat. He jumped to the ground, stooping till he was clear of the rotor blades, moving at once to the uneven ground and pulling at the creeper with his hands. Good. There were big slabs of stone. He dragged at the creeper, searching round each slab for some sign of a break in the ground. He exposed four of the stones before he found what he was looking for. It was just as Smith had told it, a hole in the ground almost closed by a great piece of stone. He stooped and put his shoulder to the stone. There was no movement. He waved to Rocco to come over. Speech was impossible against the helicopter's engines so they signed to each other. The sergeant shook his head then held up a hand and ran to the plane. He came back trailing the winch wire, wrapped it twice round the stone and clipped it back on itself. He moved Blik back a few paces and signalled Loder to start winding the winch. The wire came tight and stopped. Then the slab moved and started to tip up and over. It came upright, teetered and fell back. Blik heard nothing against the stunning sound of the plane but he felt the ground shudder under his feet. His eyes were fixed on the exposed hole and the disturbed earth and small stones running into it.

He thumbed his thanks to the sergeant and ran back to the plane. The major was turned round in his seat staring at him as if he could not believe what was happening. Blik ignored him, buckled on the belt with a torch and a climbing axe attached, put on the safety helmet and tightened the chinstrap, shouldered two coils of rope and jumped back to the ground. Back at the hole Rocco gave him an incredulous look and pointed at him then down the hole to confirm his suspicions. Blik nodded and began belaying one of the ropes round the stone slab. Rocco slapped him on the shoulder and shook his head. He ran to the plane and came back with a harness which he fitted to the president. He cleared the wire from the stone and clipped it to the back of the harness. Then he tied one end of the rope round Blik's waist and mimed to him how to tug on the rope to signal what he wanted done with the winch wire. Blik grinned and nodded. This Sergeant Rocco was bright. He would have to put in a special word for him.

Blik moved to the edge of the hole and peered down. There was nothing to see. It was just a black pit. The sergeant nodded to him. Loder had the wire wound in tight. Blik sat on the edge of the hole and ran his tongue over his lips. He slipped over the edge and had a moment of panic as he felt himself falling, then his whole body was jarred as the harness took his weight. He got his breath back. His head was just below ground level. He nodded to Rocco. He started to drop slowly down as the wire was slackened. It was suddenly dark and almost quiet, cut off from the noise of the plane. He kept one hand on the signal rope and switched on the torch with the other. He spun slowly on the end of the wire and the light of the lamp revealed the inside of the shaft. The air felt cold and damp after the heat of the sun. There were steps cut into the side of the shaft. The stone glistened with black slime. He caught the rank smell of wet fungi. The steps stopped suddenly and he saw a great gap in the wall where a whole section had broken away. Then the steps started again. Down. Down. He looked up and saw the small circle of light far above. He aimed the torch down and got a reflection. He moved the beam to and fro. Water. So the shaft was connected to the river. That made sense. Blik was suddenly keyed up, expectant. His feet touched solid ground.

He felt the wire dragging as it slacked and hung from his back. He pulled the rope to tell Rocco to lock the wire. He shone the lamp round his feet first. He was on a broad platform of rock running round the bottom of the shaft, circling the pool of water. He probed with the torch. The platform was damp and smooth, unobstructed. He walked round, shining the light on the walls. He stopped. There. There's a break in the wall, like a cave or a chamber. He went nearer. He traced the line of an arch, like the entrance to a tunnel. The light showed that inside the tunnel was blocked. He moved the torch. That was no random fall of stone. The tunnel had been blocked up with carefully laid slabs of stone. He tried to orientate himself. He decided that he was on the river side of the shaft. He checked on the pool. If that was connected to the river that would be the river's level. So the tunnel would come out just above the level of the river. He tried to remember the look of the cliff face from the river. There was no obvious place where an entrance had been blocked up. He looked at the laying of the slabs. It had been done by experts. And if they were blocking the tunnel they would take care to build up the entrance from the river so there would be no sign of a break in the face of the cliff. But why? He thought back to

Haltone's notes. Then he remembered something he had noticed when the helicopter was hovering over the cliff. From the air it was clear that the slope opposite the cliff had been terraced at one time. That explained it. Lopez had described the Pochak settlement as being on a steep terraced slope. And he had said that there was a way up the cliff across the river, a way the Pochaks had made to get on to the mountain and up to their lake of gold. Gold. Yes, what about that gold?

Blik swung the torch and stopped it at another break in the wall. He stepped round then stopped dead as the light revealed the inside of the chamber. At first glance the floor seemed occupied by a neat line of sleeping figures. He went closer. His stomach tightened. The sleeping figures were skeletons. Two had what looked like chain mail wrapped round their rib cages, another wore a rusted metal breastplate topped by a helmet. Blik reached down and lifted the helmet then dropped it and recoiled with a cry of horror. A skull grinned up at him from the stone floor. He tried to count the bodies. He made it eight or nine. He could not be certain because some of the skeletons were not complete, rotted away to nothing by damp and time and the tiny creatures that crawled in the darkness. One pair of fleshless hands clutched a crucifix.

The voice thundered in the shaft and he almost lost his balance. It took him a second or two to realise it was Rocco shouting from the top, asking if he was all right. He shouted back and retraced his steps round the platform. Everything checked. The sealed shaft, the blocked entrance from the river, the skeletons of the dead Spaniards. Everything but the gold. He had found none and there seemed no place where it could be. Wait. There was another chamber. He shone the light. Nothing but some rusting swords. A wasted journey. Proof positive that Haltone's story had been right in every detail except the bit about El Dorado.

That was the way with El Dorado. It was not a fact, it was every man's dream. He put his hand on the rope to signal Rocco and flashed the torch one last time round the walls of the shaft.

The light fell on the water as he swung the torch. His hand let go of the rope. Of course. The water. Water in here means a connection with the river. That means a way in from the river. That's where it might be, down in the water. He knelt at the edge of the pool, shining the light on the surface, then angling it to try and see down through the water. He crept round the edge, throwing the light across the pool, trying to probe its secrets. The platform narrowed as he went on till, when he was opposite his starting point, the ledge on which he knelt was only a couple of feet wide. He realised it was no use. If there was anything down in the pool it would need diving gear and underwater lights to find it. He stood up carefully and shone the light ahead. He was looking into yet another chamber. The entrance was cut back at an angle into the rock. That explained how he had missed it. From across the pool the shaft wall would seem to be solid. He stepped through the entrance. It was a smaller chamber than the others and the light showed that it had even less to offer. It was empty. He walked round it, tapping the walls with the axe, not expecting any sound other than the solid sounds he got. His foot caught and he stumbled to one knee. He swore and tracked down the obstruction, a wedge of rock close to the wall of the chamber. Or was it rock? Blik was still on his knees. He stretched out a hand and touched it. It was damp and cold like the rock. He wiped his hand across it. It was layered in slime. But it looked different, not like rock, more like roughly cast bronze. He got to his feet and stooped to lift it. It seemed very heavy for its size, at least a hundred pounds, he decided. He went down on one knee again and tapped it with the spike of the axe. A single spot of yellow light winked up at him where the point had struck. Not a wasted journey. He hit the wedge a glancing blow with the axe and a gleaming gouge opened across its surface. No, not a wasted journey. Heavy, soft, reddish yellow. Gold.

Blik swung the light round the chamber. The floor was clear of any obstruction. There can't be just one piece. A hundred pounds of gold isn't El Dorado. Wait. Not one piece; one piece left. How many others were there once? How many have you stolen, Smiddy? How many? The torch flashed round the walls seeking inspiration. Black damp stone, silent, secretive. Then a flash of light. He brought the beam back and held the spot as he stepped across. A sliver of gold shone from a ragged edge of rock up at shoulder height. He stood back and tried to guess at the quantity if that marked the other end and height of the original store of gold. Maybe twenty bars high and twenty long. Twenty times twenty. Four hundred. Four hundred times a hundred pounds. Four thousand, no, forty thousand. Forty thousand pounds' weight of gold. Good God. Almost twenty tons. Of gold. What was the price of gold? Thirty-five dollars American. Per pound? No, per ounce. Forty thousand pounds, that's sixty-four, six hundred and forty, six hundred and forty thousand ounces. Times thirty-five. It's unbelievable. He could not do the sum in his head but he knew the answer was in millions. Many millions.

He stepped back and leaned on the wall. That was crazy. That was pure guesswork. There was no proof that there had ever been all these bars. That scratch might only mean that someone had shouldered a bar and scraped it along the wall. But Lopez had said there was a lot of gold. Lopez had been right about other things. Even two hundred bars. Or a hundred. Or fifty. That scratch did prove there had been more than one. Blik wiped a hand across his face. His breath sounded loud and laboured. Shock or maybe the air was bad down there. Or maybe disgust at having found out Smith's secret. All these years of deceit. Every trip a few bars taken and carried down the river and shipped away quietly as only someone like Smith knew how. And not at thirty-five dollars an ounce. At more than that, at the free market price, or even more still in Hong Kong or India. All that fantastic fortune stowed away in numbered accounts in Switzerland and all the time the pretence of the incorruptible sailorman, the despiser of the greedy world, the protector of the primitives, the paragon of the Paradise. Alias the shit, the liar, the thief. Why, Smiddy? Why did you do it? He pressed his face against the cold wet stone. Now I've got to kill you. You know that, don't you, Smiddy? You're making me kill the only human being I ever loved, ever respected. You're making me kill him, Smiddy, because he was never there, because he was just an illusion, a trick, a filthy mean trick. Blik's disgust suddenly turned to rage. He struck wildly at the wall with the axe, ignoring the chips of stone flying back and hitting and cutting his face. He attacked the wall like a madman. Why, Smiddy? Why? Why? Why?

It was as if the stone answered his cry. Distantly at first, a growl of distaste; then nearer, a thunder of disapproval. Nearer still, like a train roaring towards him through a tunnel. Then the world shook and juddered and Blik reeled across the chamber, striking the other wall, bouncing off, stumbling, fighting to stay on his feet. His mind was back with him at the bottom of that hole in the ground. The torch searched for the entrance, the light shaking in sympathy with the rock, making focus impossible. He staggered round the chamber, feeling at the shuddering stone, trying to find the entrance. Something clawed at his face. He turned away. It wound itself round his neck. He grasped it and pulled it clear. Wire. Of course, the harness wire. There. There was a gap. He stumbled towards it. Too narrow. His body was too big to go through. The stone shook and the noise deafened him. He swung the torch up the wall. Not the entrance. Too narrow. Too high. All the way up the wall and across the roof. God. The cliff's breaking up. He staggered backwards, turning, looking for an escape from the bedlam. Suddenly he was sprawling on his back, being dragged across the shaking floor of the chamber, bruised against rock, choking for breath. Out of the chamber and then the shock of the cold water of the pool. Down, down, being spun like a top, vision blurred, all control slipping away. A steel clamp round his chest, then up and out of the water, lungfuls of breath and the noise of the moving mountain. He was soaring upwards, swinging from side to side, spinning, crashing, bouncing, assaulted by a storm of falling stones. There was no pain and the noise seemed muted. Another world. Oblivion.

Major Loder had sensed the first rumblings of the mountain up through the undercarriage into the plane. They came almost as an expected climax. He had sat at the controls for almost half an hour, watching the fuel gauge dropping towards the point of no return, fuming at Blik and his mad caper down that hole. The shaking ground made up his mind for him. He revved the engines to be ready for a quick lift. Rocco looked up at the sound and Loder signalled that he was starting to wind in the winch wire. He set the winch at full power. That'll give Mr President Sir a ride for his money. The plane shook in harmony with the ground. Loder watched Sergeant Rocco and he watched the creeper all around. When it happened it was as if the ground had been cleaved open from underneath. Loder saw the creeper split apart forty or fifty yards beyond the hole. He stared, not believing what he was seeing. The split streaked across the ground, laying open the mat of creeper, aiming straight at Rocco and the plane beyond. The major reacted instinctively, gunning the engines and giving the plane lift and forward movement to plumb the hole. He saw Rocco wrap his arms and legs round the wire as the ground opened underneath him. Twisting round, he saw the huge crack split open the ground where the plane's wheels had been a few seconds before. He put on more lift and the plane gained height, multiplying the recovery rate of the wire up out of the ground. He saw Rocco sliding back down the wire to stay close to the ground. Thank God. Blik was out and clear, hanging limp in the harness. The sergeant had his legs wrapped round Blik, his hands gripping the wire a foot or two above the harness. Loder dropped the plane slowly, keeping the winch winding in but at half speed now. He moved the plane sideways away from the yawning gap and adjusted his dropping rate to hold the two men on the wire only feet above the ground, out of danger but low enough not to be killed if they came off the wire. It was tricky. He ignored everything but the two on the end of the wire. He slowed the winch as they came up, then stopped it when they were hanging alongside the open door in the fuselage. Loder lifted the plane to give himself clearance then turned it in a steep bank to the left, putting the door under the two men. He tripped the brake on the winch and wire, harness and men dropped through the opening and sprawled inside the plane. So far, so good.

He hovered the plane and turned to see what was happening. Rocco was already on his feet, freeing the climbing rope from Blik's waist, the rope trailing out of the door. He let it go and it snaked clear and back down to the ground. The sergeant slid the door shut and locked it before nodding to Loder and holding up a thumb. His face was still a study in surprise. He turned his attention to Blik who was sitting up, taking it all in, making himself believe that he was back in the plane and safe. The light and the fresh air had brought him round as he was dragged from the hole but it was only now that the confusion was ebbing and memory flooding back. He stretched an arm, then a leg. The other arm, other leg. They all hurt but they all worked. Rocco unbuckled the harness and signed that he should stay where he was. Blik shook his head and struggled to his feet, steadying himself against the sergeant. He moved painfully up to the front of the plane and sank down in the seat next to Loder.

The major watched him dabbing at his face with a handkerchief then putting it away and fitting on his headset. You sure are a tough cookie, Mr President Sir. You look like you've been dragged through a mincer but you're sitting there making like nothing has happened. I suppose that's why presidents are presidents.

'Thank you, Major. You showed great presence of mind. The sergeant too.' The voice was not quite right but it was a very good attempt.

Loder glanced at him. 'Did you get any pigs down there, sir?'

'Yes, Major, I did. One. Bullseye.'

In a pig's eye, thought Loder. You're nuts. You didn't even have a gun.

Bilk was studying the mountain. Even scarred by the fire and the lava it looked oddly beautiful after that black shaft. He noticed little things. Three isolated strips of snow on that high escarpment. Snow? That was odd. What was snow doing several thousand feet below the snowline? 'Give her some height, Major, and slow down.'

'I'm on point of no return, sir.'

'Higher and slower, Major.' Blik picked up the binoculars and focused on his snow streaks. They seemed to have movement. And there was another. Not snow. Spurting water. Four little waterfalls spurting out of the mountain. Five. He checked round to fix the position. The plane's greater altitude helped. He had it. That escarpment was the western end of the lake. He put up the glasses again.

The waterfalls were bigger and there were more of them. The huge natural dam was leaking. Of course, these movements of the mountain. Great chunks of rock were breaking away and hurtling down. Three of the waterfalls were suddenly one and he could see more rock being ripped away by the torrent. God. That whole rock wall's going to collapse. That vast lake is going to drop down the side of the mountain. He tilted the glasses, tracing the path the water would take. It would roar down like an immense liquid avalanche and pour into the river gorges underneath where they now hovered. It would fill the gorges to the top of the cliffs and be turned and fired out as a murderous wave into the quiet water. He turned and aimed the glasses downriver, at once picking up the tall funnel glinting in the sunlight.

Loder could wait no longer. He was past his point of no return. He would probably need to use the emergency tank to make it home. He turned the plane and headed across the jungle. He noticed Blik twisting in his seat to keep the glasses trained on the quiet water below the gorges. Then he heard the hysterical voice screaming in his earphones. 'You're dead, Smiddy. You're bloody well dead. D'you hear me, Smiddy? You're dead.' In between the phrases he heard what sounded like sobs.

Chapter 7

Smith was clearing up in the galley when the helicopter circled the boat before going on up the river. He walked through to the wheelhouse and watched, seeing but unseen. He spotted the presidential crests at once. So I was right after all. It's you, Blik, making your first move in the end game. That's a typical flourish. Now get on up the river. You've met Ruth's professor, haven't you, so now you're going to check that cliff. Take your time, Blik. I won't run away. The plane finished its second circuit and headed up over the gorges as if in answer to his command. He smiled. It'll be a good game, Blik. Master versus pupil.

He moved about the boat following his morning routine. He put on a fresh pot of coffee when he heard water running in the pipes to the big cabin and had a place set in the saloon when Ruth came up. There was a shyness about their meeting, as if formal introductions should be made.

'Good morning.'

'Good morning,' said Ruth sensing the strangeness, unable in the bright light of morning to recapture the magic of the night before.

He pointed to the place at the table. 'Did you sleep well?'

'Hmm. Like a log. Is this for me?'

'Yes, I didn't know what you liked. I'll cook eggs or something if you want.'

'No, this is marvellous. Slimmer's delight,' she added, seeing the fruit juice and crispbread.

'I'll get the coffee.' He brought the jug and set it on the table.

'Aren't you having something?'

'Just coffee. I ate long ago. I get up with the sun.'

Ruth made a face. 'Lazy me. But that bed was so comfortable. I haven't slept in a bed like that for years.' She munched a piece of crispbread. 'As comfy as that, I mean. I've never ever slept in a bed quite like that.'

Smith grinned and poured the coffee. 'I'll leave you to have your breakfast in peace. I'll take mine through to the wheelhouse.'

'Wait,' she said, swallowing. 'I'll come too if that's all right. I'd like some air. It's a bit sticky in here.'

'It's the humidity. It gets worse farther down in the swamps.'

They carried their cups through and laid them on the window ledge. Little breaths of air puffed through the open windows.

'Oh, it's beautiful, Smithy. So quiet. So peaceful.'

He sipped his coffee.

'Was I imagining things or did I hear an aeroplane when I was getting up?'

'There was a plane. One of yours.'

'Mine?'

'American Army. Helicopter. They're building a base.'

'Where? Not here surely.'

'No. At the capital.'

'It was a long way from home, here, I mean.'

'Having a look at the mountain, I suppose. Seeing what the fire has done. It was one of the planes they've lent to the president.' He drained his cup. 'There it is now.' He laid down the cup and pointed. 'There, over the gorges.' His head was full of questions. What did you find, Blik? Did you find the way in from the clifftop? Did you find that one piece I left behind last time, the piece I couldn't reach yesterday? Maybe that's why I left it, so you could find it, so we could have it out at last, you and me. You're flying away now so it's my move. I've only got one and you know it; down the river. So the place is chosen, the estuary. You choose the weapons, Blik.

'Listen, Smithy.'

At first he thought it was the distant whirring of the plane's rotors coming back on some freak current of air.

'Oh look. Isn't that fantastic?'

The whirring was from birds' wings; not a few birds, all the birds of the forest and the jungle. They were rising in ones and twos, in dozens, in huge flocks. They scattered colour across the green of the jungle then up and across the sky as they rose and wheeled and swooped and fluttered. There were yellow crested cockatoos, pairs of hornbills, crowds of brilliant lories, packs of parrots, solitary herons, black and white river eagles, hordes of bee and honey eaters, clusters of birds of paradise, and diving, gliding, zooming squadrons of swallows from the cliffs bordering the quiet water. The threshing of their wings was the rhythm section behind the weird discordant melody of the squawking, screaming, honking, chirruping beaks. The noise was stunning and the countless flying shapes shattered the sun's light into mesmeric moving patterns on the water and the ship's deck.

Smith did not wait to admire the birds. He went up the foredeck at the double and started the windlass, wound it into gear and swung off the brake. The anchor cable jerked and started to heave in. He looked over the side and saw it was leading ahead. He ran back to the wheelhouse and thumbed the starters on the main engines. He lost the starting whine in the dreadful noise from the sky but felt the vibrations through the hull as both diesels fired.

Ruth turned, realising something was happening, her eyes still big with awe at the birds. Her mouth opened but the words were lost.

Smith put his mouth close to her ear and shouted. 'We're getting to hell out of here.'

Her soundless lips asked why.

'Because I've spent a lifetime up here and I've never seen this before. When that happens I run for cover.'

He moved the throttles ahead to take *Mermaid* up to her anchor and left Ruth frowning as he ran up for'ard again. He watched the clanking chain, willing it to come in faster. He gave no thought to what it all might mean. These birds spelled mortal danger and everything he did was ordered by his instinct to survive. Chain up and down, anchor off the bottom. Come on, let's see you. Shackle, shank, flukes. He whirled on the brake and spun the windlass out of gear, leaving the anchor hanging outside the hawse pipe. That would do for now. He sprinted back midships and pushed both throttles to full power. A moment's hesitation then the boat's stern squatted down into the water as both propellers bit at full revs. He spun the wheel hard to starboard. Ruth was pointing. He crinkled his eyes against the light. What looked like plumes of black smoke were rising from the jungle. He grabbed the glasses with one hand. Christ. He leaned close to Ruth. 'Flying foxes. Thousands of them. Tens of thousands. Bats. They don't fly in the day. Never.'

The boat was curving round in a tight circle, cutting a huge wake on the smooth water. He took Ruth's arm and pulled her behind the wheel. He stood behind her and shouted instructions. 'You steer for a bit.' He eased the wheel and put her hands on the spoke ends. 'Just like yesterday. Remember?' He spun the wheel to midships. The sweeping bow slowed. He found his marker and steadied *Mermaid* on course. 'That big tree. The biggest one. Right ahead. D'you see it?' She nodded. 'Good girl. Just keep her heading straight for it.' His eyes swept along the engine dials. OK. He ran up to the bow, put the windlass in gear and eased the brake. With the engines at full power the boat was planing up, her two big side keels making her a crude hydroplane. The anchor had turned inboard so he had to lower it into the water and spin it. It took three attempts before he got it tight home into the hawse pipe. He dropped on the big claw and wound the bottle screw tight.

The armada of birds was falling astern, spreading out, finding space but still staying in the air, making no attempt to land. Smith went back midships and took the wheel from Ruth. 'You're the most useful passenger I've had for a long time.'

'Smithy, I'm scared.'

'That makes two of us.'

The pattern of noise was changing, the ship dominating with the racing engines, the roaring exhausts, the rush of cut and threshed water and the buffeting wind of *Mermaid*'s speed. The sound of the birds was already faint behind the ship noises. But there was something else, vague, indefinable, ominous. It was a sensation, an aura. Smith felt the hair bristling behind his ears. He looked back. Nothing. Just the wheeling birds in the air and the dying wake of the boat on the water. What the hell is it? Where is it? Maybe I'm running straight into it, not away from it. That helicopter. Something Blik's started? No, that's not his way. He'd have to be here. Smith's eyes searched the water and the banks. They stopped on a group of huts on the south bank, standing clear of the ground on long stilts like a covey of wading birds. Deserted. Even at that distance he knew the village was deserted. There were no canoes. So the river people had gone. That meant floods. He swept the sky. Not a cloud in sight. No clouds, no flash floods. So why had the river men loaded their canoes and paddled away up the creeks towards the higher ground? The drums. He remembered the frantic messages of the drums. Idiot. After all these years you should know to take these people seriously. But it was the mountain they drummed about; the lava flowed and the mountain burned. That meant nothing down here. He looked back again. His eyes narrowed as he traversed along the cliffs beyond the smooth water then opened wide in disbelief as they came to the gorges.

Ruth was beside him. Her fears had grown as she watched Smith and sensed his apprehension. If he was worried, here on his river, she knew there was reason to be afraid. The lack of evident danger only made it worse. What awful thing could throw these thousands of birds up into the sky? What awful thing could make this fearless man run scared? She followed his eyes round and astern. Her unpractised eyes saw nothing but one glance at Smith told her that he now knew what the thing was and where it was coming from.

That first sweep along the cliffs had shown him water cascading, turning the cliffs into a crescent shaped waterfall. Water where he knew there was no water. Then at the gorges he saw what looked like water but couldn't be water for it filled the gorge from side to side and up and over the top of the sheer rock walls. A hundred and fifty feet high and the same across. He turned to check the boat's course then turned back. It was water and it was already exploding out of the gorge like an immense beast leaping for freedom from its cage. Its roar reached out ahead of it. The aura, the sensation was gone. There was just the rising thunder of doom. The lake. It had to be the lake. He saw Ruth, eyes big, face pale, transfixed. He grabbed her and spun her round. 'It's the lake,' he shouted. 'The lake on the mountain.' She made no sign. She seemed to have no senses, no sight, no speech, no hearing. He held the wheel with one hand and with the other shook her like a terrier shaking a rat till the spell broke and her eyes came alive and she started to fight back. 'That's better. Over there. That locker. Life jackets.' He pushed her so hard that she reeled across the wheelhouse and crashed into the locker. She held on for a few seconds then opened the locker and dragged out the jackets. Smith took one and slipped it on, jamming the wheel with his knee while he tied the tapes. He saw her copying his movements. She started to turn her head as if drawn against her will to stare back at the water. He took a fistful of hair and twisted her head to face the bow. 'Eyes front, girlie. Stay right beside me and do exactly what I say.'

He turned and looked back up the river. His stomach clamped itself into a knot. The first explosion of water from the gorge had hit the river and spread from bank to bank. But stoked from behind with a vast supply of fuel it had rolled the river up into a massive wave, its front slope soaring up to an angry crest, overhanging, falling and tumbling down the slope, being replaced by a new crest, a huge moving mountain of water, bellowing with rage, flexing, stretching, reaching out for its prey, eating up the distance to the fleeing boat with a giant's appetite. Smith thought he had maybe two minutes. The only hope was to get off the river. Nothing could live through the front of that wave. He tore his eyes away and watched *Mermaid's* bow. It was a chilling contrast; the beautiful flare of the bow, the delicate spume arching up and away with the speed of the boat, the smooth water ahead and the lush green of the jungle beyond. That, and closing fast astern the wild beast that would strike, smash, swallow, then scatter a pitiful excrement in its wake.

The creek that ran in just beyond the first bend was the only chance and a very slim one at that. Smith held the boat across the bend at full throttle. He would need time. He dare not take the boat into the creek at full power. With her stern squatted deep into the water she would almost certainly take the ground and lie like a staked goat for the springing tiger. He forced himself not to look back again. The swelling crescendo from astern marked the dwindling time. He saw Ruth standing stiffly erect, her hands clutching the window ledge, the knuckles white, the muscles of her neck bulging as they fought to stop herself looking back. The high bow shut out any view of the water ahead. *Mermaid* seemed to be racing straight into the jungle with its tangle of pandanus and creeper and the tall palms and hardwoods beyond. The mouth of the creek opened into view from under the sweep of the bow. Smith held his course and speed, opening up the creek on the port side, praying there was enough water so close to the bank for the boat's squatted stern. His right hand hovered over the controls. Now. It was not a time to be kind to the engines. He slammed them both straight through to full astern and felt rather than heard the screaming gear down in the hull. *Mermaid* slowed as if brakes had been kicked on and held down. The bow dipped sharply and for an awful second Smith thought she had touched bottom. Then the boat trimmed herself. He wound the wheel hard over to port, saw the bow swing, brought the engines to stop then ahead at quarter power. With way still on her the boat swung quickly and he steadied her up for the mouth of the creek.

Mermaid was now broadside on to the wave. Smith flashed a glance to port then dragged his terrified eyes back to the bow and what he now knew to be an almost hopeless chance of survival. He grabbed Ruth and pulled her round to his right side, putting himself between her and the wave. He did it without thinking but a tiny corner of his brain screamed with unkind laughter. It'll take more than that to save her, Smithy. In the split second he had looked left he had seen the whole wave in all its dreadful splendour. Its front was concave, brown streaked with white foam, thin mud rather than water, and it swept up to a boiling crest fifty or sixty feet above the river. The crest boiled white and drooled down the front curve like a salivating monster while above it huge boulders and trees tossed like ping pong balls on the fountains in a shooting gallery. From its peak in mid-river the wave sloped down and backwards in a broad arrowhead, its edges trailing it along the banks, submerging them, overflowing them and raging on into the jungle, clawing and demolishing everything in its path. The noise did not just stun the ears. It seemed to have a visual quality, its thunder vibrating the eyes, pushing images out of focus. The edge of the arrowhead was two hundred yards away upriver. About five seconds.

Mermaid was in the mouth of the creek. Smith risked half power. One second. The creek was narrow, the jungle growing within a few yards on both sides. Two seconds. A quick look astern showed the leading edge of the wave abreast the creek in the middle of the river, immensely high, venomous, lethal. Three seconds. The boat was twenty yards into the creek, the lush jungle to left and right looking like safety, the lie brutally underscored by the bedlam from the river. Four seconds. Smith reached out and pulled Ruth in behind him, guiding her hands round to clasp together on his chest. He half turned. Her face was pale, the flesh tight, eyes misted. He shouted against the din. 'It's going to be rough. Hold on tight.' Five seconds.

The edge of the wave swept past the mouth of the creek, hesitated as it found a new path to explore, broke off and surged into the narrow channel, filling it, overflowing, swelling up and submerging the jungle, driving on and catching the escaping boat. It hit and broke against the stern, kicking the boat ahead, throwing her off course, the brown water sweeping along her length, tearing at fixtures, searching out apertures, spilling through doorways, up and through window spaces, fouling everything with brown slime. But the weight behind the water pushed it down and under the boat, scooping *Mermaid* up like a plaything, balancing her on its crest, rolling and pitching the boat left and right, up and down in the humps and hollows behind the crest as the water raced ahead, fed more power every second as the lake emptied itself down the mountain into the river and on out across the jungle.

It was only having the wheel to hold on to that let Smith keep his feet as the boat plunged and reared and fought to stay alive in the moving maelstrom. He just clung to the wheel, making no attempt to control direction and speed, knowing that *Mermaid* was already high above the ground, seeing the jungle ahead then seeing water as the jungle disappeared under the spreading sea. Vision was a confused blur of oddly assorted images. An uprooted tree dancing alongside, the sky blue and tranquil, a soaring cliff of brown water, hands that were not his clutched under his chin, an open doorway, a doorway full of water, water up to his waist then only a puddle of water sloshing round his feet, the top of a tree sticking up through the water outside, the sky again, locker doors bursting open and spewing gear across the deck, a face reflected in the shining brass of the binnacle, a yawning canyon with a stand of hardwoods growing up through the far slope. The boat swept down into the trough, spun like a top, steadied then surged into the cluster of trees. The darkness was sudden and almost complete as the boat hurtled through the tangle of branches, carving a path but being snagged and slowed. Branches swept along the boat's deck, snapping off against obstructions; others swept higher, raking along the top of the deckhouse, tearing out halyards and aerials, buckling vents, assaulting the funnel, snapping its guys, throwing it down across the stern to splinter the dinghy hanging in its davits. The noise of destruction overcame the noise of the water. *Mermaid* slowly gave up the fight against the trees and lay trapped as the flood rolled past her. But the water made one last try to tear her loose. The lump of water she had slipped down into the trees followed her and broke over her with an angry roar then flowed on leaving the boat even more tightly enmeshed in the high branches.

The sudden braking as the boat charged the trees doubled Smith over, driving the spokes of the wheel into his stomach, winding him, making him lose his hold. His feet slid on the slimy deck and, as the boat bucked, he was thrown across the wheelhouse to crash against a locker and be dumped in a heap on the deck. As the boat was caught and brought to a halt he slid about on the slime grasping for holds to haul himself back to his feet. Then water burst in from all angles and his nightmare was reality again. There was water in his mouth, in his nostrils, all over and around him. His chest was being crushed in a vice. Lights exploded inside his head, a galaxy of colour, a dazzle of shapes. There was no pain. There was nothing.

It was like that last time, all these years ago. Dull pain through his body, sounds inside his head, and a swirling mist in front of his eyes. Someone leaning over him. A Jap soldier? No, that had just been fear. Fingers on his forehead, down across his cheek; warm breath and a woman's voice. A woman? Of course, that was the Omar Khayyam bit. A Jug of Wine, a Loaf of Bread—and Thou beside me singing in the Wilderness—Oh Wilderness were Paradise enow. Paradise. Paradise Smith. That's me. But it wasn't a woman, it was a boy. A half-caste boy with blue eyes. Blik. Is that you, Blik? No, it couldn't be Blik. That was long ago. Blik was in a helicopter now. Blik was going to kill him. The mist swirled and cleared. So it was true. This time he really was dead. He was lying there dead and the mermaid was there looking after him. She wasn't carved out of wood now; she was real, alive, breathing. As he had died, she had come alive. She was wet too, just risen out of the water. Why was she wearing a life jacket? That was ridiculous. Mermaids don't wear lifejackets. Water. Of course, there had been a lot of water. Mountains of it, and valleys and ridges. Dirty slimy brown water. Everywhere. And trees growing out of the sea, then trees all round and over the boat. His boat. And this was his wheelhouse. There was the wheel and the binnacle. But what was that tree doing growing through the window? He didn't grow trees in his wheelhouse. The mermaid's lips were moving but he couldn't hear the words for the roar of rushing water in his ears. And the mermaid's eyes were the wrong colour. They were brown. They should be green. That was how he painted them, green. He was looking over the bow, recognising that the figurehead was the twin of a woman called Ruth Carter. It all came back in a rush. The birds, the wave, the creek, the trees. So he wasn't dead after all. And the mermaid was Ruth Carter.

'Hallo,' she said.

He struggled up to a sitting position and leaned his back against the bulkhead. 'Hallo to you too.' He shook his head and explored with his fingers till he found the tender spot on the back of his head. He stretched out a hand and held it against Ruth's cheek. 'So you're real then. And we came through that thing alive?'

She nodded. 'Seems so though I can hardly believe it myself. I don't know how you did it, Smithy.'

'You and me both.' He peered up at the branch. 'What the hell's that doing in here? Where the devil are we anyway?'

'I don't know. Don't care either. We're alive. That's good enough for me.'

'I suppose you're right.' He got to his feet and hung on to the doorframe. His eyes focused on the engine controls. That's funny. Engines are stopped but all the switches are on. I can't remember stopping the engines. So the water's shorted out all the electrics. He let himself slide across with the heel of the boat and closed all the switches. 'Come on

110

then, Miss Carter. Let's find out where we are and why we're still alive.'

They hauled themselves up the sloping deck and came out on the high side. There were branches everywhere, forcing them to duck their heads as they moved along the deck. The foliage and the decks were steaming as the heat dried away the water but the boat was in dappled shade under its screen of leaves. Smith looked at his watch. The second hand was still sweeping. So the advertisements didn't lie. It was not yet noon. He climbed up to the monkey island, forcing his way past a branch. There was some sort of view from up there. Close to, it was a view of wreckage. Everywhere he looked along the length of the boat there were smashed fittings and tangles of rope and wire. The topmast had disappeared and the funnel was lying flat across the stern. Through the tops of the trees there was a vista of water. No ground anywhere. Just water and, here and there, trees sticking up through it. He clambered back down and fought his way to the rail. Water there too, flowing past but the level dropping as he watched.

'Well?' asked Ruth.

'Well what?'

'Well, where are we?'

'We seem to be up a tree. Several in fact.'

'I can see that but . . .'

The boat lurched and dropped several feet, its weight smashing the branches, stopping when it settled again in the water. A freed branch lashed out across the deck and knocked Ruth and Smith sprawling. They finished up with their heads close together.

'And we seem to be coming down now,' said Smith. He got back on to his feet and offered Ruth his hand. 'Let's get inside. Maybe there are fewer trees in there.'

The saloon was in deep shade. He found a torch that still worked in the wheelhouse. Everything was coated with brown slime but the water had drained away. He started down the stair to the main cabin but was stopped half-way. That was where the water had drained. The torch showed the water two feet deep in the room, the surface littered with wreckage. He turned back up to the saloon and walked to the table. He drew his fingers along the surface he had planed and sanded and polished till it shone like a mirror. His fingers came away thick with mud. He looked slowly round, realising that every corner of the boat would be thus fouled. He swore quietly and hammered his fist on the table. Then he hit the table with all his strength, then again and again, shouting oaths at the top of his voice in time with his fist. He felt better after a while. His hand hurt and he shook it to ease the pain. He went across and leaned on one of the window ledges. A cockatoo floundered clumsily down out of the sky and perched on a branch. Its breast was heaving with the unaccustomed exertion of staying aloft so long and its yellow crest erected and flattened in indignation. It peered at Smith and managed to summon up an angry scream. 'Quite right too,' he told it. 'Shocking language, wasn't it? Go on, you tell me off. I deserve it.' The bird moved to and fro on the branch, screeching at him and ruffling its plumage angrily. Smith started to laugh. The bird screeched furiously. Smith was suddenly convulsed with laughter. The bird was incensed, prancing up and down, screaming at him. It got so angry that it missed its perch and had to flutter awkwardly to regain its balance. This provoked Smith to more hysterical laughter. He staggered away from the window and slumped down in one of the swivel chairs that ringed the table. He swung the chair round and held his feet up while it spun. When it stopped he stuck his legs out and sat looking at his toes. He wriggled them and nodded. Beyond them he saw a pair of feet, a pair of legs in wet slacks. His eyes crept up, frowning at the lifejacket, looking down at his own, then up again till they rested on Ruth's face. 'Hallo, Queen Victoria. I see we are not amused.'

'I wouldn't say that. I'm just wondering what's going to happen to us.'

'Don't worry. Smithy'll think of something.'

'That helicopter. The American one. Maybe it will look for us.'

Smith gave her a crooked smile. 'Yes, it'll look for us. It'll look for us till it finds us. But it won't help us. It'll just watch and wait.'

'That's crazy. Of course it'll help.'

Smith shook his head. 'No. Just watch and wait, that's what it'll do. I know it doesn't make sense but, trust me, that's what's going to happen.'

Ruth's patience was exhausted. Shock was catching up with her. There was a tremor in her voice. 'Smithy, what are we going to do?'

He got up and put his hands on her shoulders. 'First we're going to take off these goddam lifejackets. And then, well I don't know about you, Mermaid, but me, I'm going to find me a bottle somewhere in this wreck and I'm going to get stoned right out of my mind.'

He used his lifejacket to wipe the mud off two chairs and one end of the table. He held a chair for Ruth but she made no move. He shrugged and went over and opened the sideboard. 'Here we are.' He held up a bottle. 'Just what the doctor ordered. Malt Scotch. Painkiller supreme.' He sat down in his usual chair at the head of the table and set out two glasses. He spun the cap off the bottle and flicked it through the window where the cockatoo was composing itself. 'Will you join the captain in a little noggin, Miss Carter?'

'No, thanks. I only drink to celebrate.'

'Hear hear to that.' He half-filled one tumbler. 'The toast is to life. Isn't that worth celebrating? You said it yourself.

We're still alive.'

'I'll take a raincheck on mine till we're rescued.'

Smith took a long swallow. 'Aaah.' He licked his lips. 'Do please sit down at least. I'm getting a crick in my neck looking up at you.'

She peeled off her lifejacket. 'I don't suppose there are any dry clothes on board.'

'I don't suppose so. Don't worry. In this heat you'll soon steam dry. By then of course you'll be soaked again with sweat. I beg your pardon, perspiration.'

She sat down angrily. 'And you'll be soaked with whisky.'

'Let's hope so.' He took another gulp.

She leaned across the table. 'Smithy, please, isn't there something we can do?'

'Mermaid, you don't seem to approve but I'm doing the most sensible thing there is to do.' He emptied the glass and set it on the table, waving her to silence. 'The tiger chased us through the jungle. We escaped up a tree. We have to stay treed till the tiger goes away. When he goes away, that'll be time enough for us to think about getting out of here.' The boat jerked and settled and he steadied the bottle and the glasses. 'That tiger's going to take some time to go away. Maybe till it's dark. Maybe longer than that. So there's nothing we can do at least till daylight tomorrow.' He refilled the glass. 'Cheers, Mermaid.'

'Stop calling me Mermaid.'

He sipped the Scotch. 'Of course, you don't know.'

'Know what?'

'Know about the mermaid. The figurehead. The mermaid the boat's called after.' He frowned. 'Wonder how she is? Must have been rough for her.'

'What about the figurehead?'

Smith looked up. 'Oh yes. Well, don't you think it's odd? I carved her with my own hands just about the time you were born. No model. Just out of my head. And you're her spitting image. Except your eyes. Your eyes are the wrong colour. They should have been green.'

Ruth was taken off guard. 'I'm—I'm sorry about my eyes.'

'No, no. No, no.' He took a drink. 'Your eyes are better. I admit I got that wrong.'

'And the tail, of course.'

He grinned. 'Yes, that too. You've got a much better tail.'

She laughed and told him to stop being a fool. But she felt warm inside. It seemed to break the tension that had held her since that race down the river and into the creek, then the terror of the wave and the boat bucking and rearing till it crashed to a stop in the trees and the water had poured in and over her. She realised Smith was relieving his tension with the whisky . . . 'I'm hungry,' she announced.

'Try the galley.' He emptied and refilled his glass. He seemed to be immune to the alcohol.

She came back with hard-boiled eggs and tinned asparagus, biscuits, butter, and a can of orange juice. 'That was clever of you, Smithy, to have all these eggs ready in the fridge.'

'Old sailor's trick. Easiest quick meal there is.' He took an egg and made it disappear in his hands, produced it from his ear, made it disappear again, leaned across and pulled it from behind Ruth's neck, then popped it into his mouth, bringing it out again with half of it bitten away. 'Damn it, Smith, you're not supposed to eat the props,' he scolded.

Ruth laughed and helped herself to food. He ate and drank and talked. That seemed to be the only effect of the whisky. He talked. He talked about the boat and the dinner parties he gave. He drew cruel caricatures in words of his guests, government officials, businessmen, planters, their wives, the girls from Orange Street. He talked about the island and the river. He talked about the tribes. He talked about the world beyond the island and why he never went there. He talked about life. Never about death. The first bottle was replaced by a second. Ruth liked him for taking her mind off their predicament. As she listened she realised that he had spent a lifetime on the island not just loving what he was doing but finding answers to questions most people never thought of asking. But she sensed there were things he didn't talk about, secret things that even the whisky did not pry from him. There was no discussion. He asked and answered all the questions.

The afternoon wore on. The heat was stifling. Smith talked and drank and talked, never once failing to save the bottle as *Mermaid* lurched and crashed downwards as the flood slowly subsided. The last drop came late when the sun was low and the light almost gone from the saloon. Smith listened to the crash of breaking branches, the creak then the roar of falling trees, the screech of wood on metal. He waited till all was quiet again then got slowly to his feet and stood for a few seconds testing his balance. He went out on to the deck and peered over the side. He came back in, splashed some whisky into a clean glass and then emptied the bottle into his own. He held the smaller drink out to Ruth. 'Miss Carter, I am happy to announce that we have just landed at an unknown destination. There will be an overnight halt for refuelling and maintenance.' He touched glasses then drained his in a single gulp. Before Ruth could taste the whisky, Smith crumpled on to the deck, settled in an untidy heap and immediately began snoring contentedly.

Chapter 8

Ruth woke with the sun on her face. She closed her eyes again at once and wondered why they were sore. She put up a hand and felt the huge swelling the mosquitoes had left. She felt sore all over. She lay still and thought back over the night. She had had a bad time.

It had started with a laugh. Smith's sudden surrender to the whisky had been funny. She remembered someone saying that you never knew a man till you'd seen him drunk. She had tried moving him but he was a dead weight so she put a cushion under his head and sat watch over him. The darkness, when it came, had been complete. There was no light at all till late on when the moon rose and little of that penetrated to the boat trapped amid the trees. The night sounds were frightening. The flood seemed to have left a lot of things still alive. Smith's snoring made her angry and she shouted at him then got down and shook him to try and stop it. He snuffled and turned over and started snoring again. In the end she lay down and put an arm round him. That was better. She felt less alone. Then he turned and breathed on her face. Ugh. She rolled away. The deck made a hard bed. There were insects everywhere. The night was a long memory of pain and imagined fears and sleeplessness.

She opened her eyes again and peered around. She was on one of the settees in Smith's den. How had she got in there? She could not remember. She sat up and swung her legs on to the deck. Smells started reaching her. The putrid smell of mud and stagnant water, the smell of her own body, her clothes streaked with brown slime and wet with sweat. But there was also the smell of fresh coffee and that got her to her feet. She followed it unsteadily through the empty saloon to the galley. A hatch was open in the deck and she could see Smith's back down there bent over some machinery. She took down a mug and filled it with coffee from the jug on the stove.

Smith's head came up through the hatch. He started to say 'Good morning' but cut himself off short. 'You look even worse than I feel, Miss Carter.'

She nodded her head and sipped her coffee.

He climbed up and poured a mug for himself. 'I won't ask you if you slept well.'

'No, don't. But will you promise me something?'

'Anything.'

'Next time you decide to get stoned, take me along. You look as fresh as a daisy.'

'I did invite you, didn't I?'

'You did.'

He drank some coffee and studied her. 'Is there anything I should apologise for?'

Ruth summoned up a small smile. 'No. No, you were a perfect gentleman, Smithy. Come to think of it, that's an odd way to describe a drunk but you know what I mean.'

'Hmm. Didn't think I could have forgotten.'

'Is that some kind of compliment?' she asked.

He thought about it. 'Yes, I suppose it is.' He put down his mug and lifted a sponge from a basin of water in the sink. 'Here, let me swab those eyes for you.' He wiped her face and held a sponge against the swellings. 'How's that?'

'Better.' She took the sponge from him and continued the treatment.

'Mosquitoes,' he explained. 'They've got good taste. They leave me alone.' He drained his coffee and refilled the mug. 'I'm afraid things are going to be a bit primitive for a while.

We'll have to save the water for cooking and drinking. But I'll have the generator working soon so we'll have lights and fans for tonight and I'll rig up new screens to keep all these bugs at bay.'

'You make it sound as if we're still going to be here to-night.' She looked around. 'Where are we anyway?'

He beckoned and she followed him outside. It was a shock. There were high trees all round. She looked over the side. *Mermaid* lay on a tangle of fallen trees, broken branches and undergrowth. The only water in sight lay in pools showing through from under the bush. She looked aft down a path carved through the trees by the boat. Beyond there was jungle and pools left on the uneven ground by the flood. Over the bow the sun shone between trees on the edge of the copse. A few more yards and the boat would have broken free and been carried on by the wave to God knows where. But that's where we are, she thought. God knows where. What good's a boat without water? She stared at the trees and the jungle, all steaming in the boiling sun. 'Where's the river?' she asked.

'Over there.' He waved vaguely to starboard.

'How far?'

'That depends.' He pointed aft. 'That's the way we came; two, maybe three miles.' He waved at the trees on the beam. 'It bends away from us that way. Four miles.' He pointed out over the starboard bow. 'That's the way we'll go. It's not much more than half a mile. There's a long creek that runs into the river.'

'If that's the shortest walk, that's for me. What do we do when we get there?'

'We sail down the river to the sea and round the coast to Port Bancourt.'

Ruth wiped the sweat from her face and neck. 'How do you know we'll find a boat there? You're not going to try

119

and take a native canoe all that way, are you? Will there be any canoes? Won't they all have been smashed or swept away?'

'Who said anything about a canoe? What's wrong with *Mermaid*?'

She shut her eyes and shook her head to try and clear her brain. 'Let's just recap. I've missed something. I'm not properly awake. It's half a mile to this creek. So how can we sail *Mermaid* down the river? We're in the middle of the jungle. There's no water. A boat does need water, doesn't it?'

'Usually.'

'So how do we get *Mermaid* to the river? Are you going to put wheels on her and drive her out?'

'Something like that.'

Ruth leaned on the rail. 'Smithy, are you still drunk? Or is this your idea of a joke? It's too early in the morning for me.'

He put a hand on her shoulder. 'I'm not drunk. It's not a joke. You and me, Ruth, we're going to take this boat across that jungle back to the river.'

She looked at him for a long time. 'I do believe you mean it.'

'That's better.' He took her arm. 'Come inside and I'll show you how.' He sat her at the table in the saloon and came back with a pad of paper, ripping off damp sheets till he came to dry ones. 'Bloody water got everywhere.'

'Is there any more coffee?' she asked.

He came back with two full mugs. He sat down. 'I was like you, Ruth, when I went out there and saw how things were. Then I went down to see how the hull was. She's a tough old girl. She seems tight. Bit of damage here and there. One of the propeller shafts is badly bent but I can fix that. It was when I saw how she was lying that I got the answer. She's got a tree right under her just about midships and she's lying with her bow on the ground and her stern up in the air. As I looked at her I remembered launching rowing boats as a kid. They were too heavy to move on the beach. But with a couple of rollers under them even a kid could trundle them into the water.'

'I still don't get it, Smithy. This isn't a row boat, this is a ship.'

'Right. So we need pretty big rollers. D'you think tree trunks might be big enough? Here, let me show you.' He pulled over the pad and started sketching. 'This is the boat. We'll put a couple of trees under her and a few more out ahead of her. We lay out both anchors ahead like that, then we start heaving on the anchors. *Mermaid* rolls along on the logs.' He finished the drawing. 'Then we start again. Lay out the anchors, cut more logs. She'll stay upright because of her side keels. They and the bar keel will take the weight all right. They're strong. She's accustomed to taking the ground. I made them that way for some of the places round the coast where the only safe place is to run her up on the beach at high tide and let her take the ground when the tide drops.'

Ruth was staring at the drawing. 'It looks so simple.'

'It won't be.' He sounded doubtful. 'But it's our only chance.' He beat the table slowly with a clenched fist. 'It's got to work.'

She put out a hand and stopped the fist. 'It'll work, Smithy.'

He smiled at her. 'That's my girl. I'm going to need your help.' He swallowed his coffee in a gulp. 'Now, first things first. I'll get the generator started then the pumps going and pump her out. Maybe you'll tidy up a bit in here and in the galley. I'll draw these two propellers and get them on deck. They'll only get damaged more than they already are if I leave them on. When that's done you can help me shift the ballast.'

'How do we do that? And why?'

'It's pig iron. It's in the hold. When I'd refitted the boat I found that, with all the new machinery and fuel tanks being aft, she floated with her bow up like a speedboat. For the river she has to be flat so I keep the pigs in the fore end to trim her down.' He tore off the used page of the pad. 'Now she's lying like this with her bow down. If we lay out the anchors and heave on them, she'll dig her bow right into the ground. So we have to get the bow up to let us get logs underneath the fore end. If we take the ballast out of the hold and stow it aft, in the lazaret, that should tip her on the tree that's underneath her.' He drew another sketch on top of the first one. 'Stern down, bow up, and we're in business.'

Ruth nodded slowly. 'I'm convinced, Smithy. My head tells me it's the craziest thing ever. But I think you'll do it.'

'We'll do it.'

'I have one question.'

'Fire ahead.'

'Before we start, can I have a bath?'

He lay back in his chair and laughed. 'That's what I like to hear. A woman with her priorities right.'

'There never was a man who understood what a bath means to a woman.'

'All right. One bucket of water.'

She gripped his hand. 'Thanks, Smithy. You'll see. It'll be worth it. I'll work twice as hard.'

She was as good as her word. She started in the galley, rearranging the tumbled contents of all the lockers, feeling hungry as she stacked cans and packets, but not stopping to eat. With the generator working, the pumps had drained all the water from the inside of the boat so she started on the main cabin. The carpet was sopping wet. She folded it as best she could and struggled it up the stairway to the saloon and out on deck. Mattress, sheets and quilt followed, then all the clothes in the drawers and wardrobes. She spread them on the deck, on the main hatch cover, hung the clothes over the rails till *Mermaid* took on the look of the yard behind a Chinese laundry. She mopped up puddles of water trapped in corners and used the wet cloths to clean the furniture in the saloon. The smell of the mud clung everywhere but she killed it when she found an insecticide spray. It was only when she stopped to admire her work and sniff the disinfected air that she realised her clothes were soaked with sweat. The hum of the generator gave her inspiration. She switched on the overhead fans and stood under one, letting the breeze refresh her. Suddenly she was back home in the States, up in the mountains, with the buzz and snarl of the lumberjacks' chain saws in her ears.

She went out and looked over the side. It was Smith trimming branches off the tree on which the boat lay. He handled the big saw as if it had no weight but when he started to cut she could see the muscles of his bent back rippling as he held the bar with its whirling chain into the wood. With the saw stopped, the noises of the jungle seemed more obvious than before. Insects hummed and clicked and the returned birds squawked and cheeped and whistled. Ruth watched Smith hauling away the cut branches and chopping at the creeper with a machete. He worked with a demon energy that was frightening. She realised that getting *Mermaid* back to the river was not for him just a hope. It was a necessity. It sprang from loyalty to this thing he had built with his own hands. She envied the boat. To be loved that much, to inspire that amount of effort and courage, that really was something.

He shouted up to her. 'Looks like washday up there.'

Ruth waved and watched him cutting his way through the undergrowth, up to beyond the bow. She saw him sizing up one of the big hardwoods. The saw snarled as he pulled the engine to life, pop-popped as he let it idle while he found good holds for his feet, then roared and rasped as he angled it into the trunk. It was just like in the mountains back home, she thought. Except that it wasn't back home and the man wasn't working for a wage. Smith was manufacturing survival. He moved his position and sliced in straight, joining up with the first cut, completing the notch and knocking out the wedge of wood. He moved round the trunk and started on the first of the felling cuts. Three sweeping cuts into the trunk and he killed the engine and stepped clear. The tree stood defiantly erect then tilted, creaked, sagged and crashed to the ground with a roar of breaking branches and a great swishing of leaves. It lay ahead of *Mermaid*, across her path, the first of her makeshift wheels. The saw burped and bellowed as Smith moved in to lop the branches and slice the trunk into two huge logs. Ruth felt the sun on her head. It was high now, clear of the tree tops and blazing down mercilessly. She went back inside and stood under one of the fans.

She found more jobs to do as the saw buzzed angrily. She counted two more trees falling, feeling their impact up through the hull from the ground. She wondered how Smith kept it up out there in the full glare of the sun. She was already weak with the heat, all energy sapped. She was collapsed in a chair under the fan when he came back on board.

He was in high spirits. 'That was a good morning's work.' He fetched a towel and started mopping off the perspiration. 'You've been busy too, I see. It's all starting to look quite ship-shape.' He went through to the galley and came back with a big pitcher of water. 'You're all in, aren't you?'

She nodded weakly.

'Salt, my girl. You need salt.' He took a big jar from the sideboard, opened it, and sprinkled yellow pills on the table. He got glasses and filled them from the pitcher. He pushed a handful of pills into his mouth and swallowed them, washed them down with water and refilled his glass. 'Come on. Your turn now. You won't taste a thing. They're sugar coated.'

She took one and swallowed it.

'Keep going. Half a dozen and lots of water. Same again every couple of hours. It goes straight through you in this weather, the salt. See.' He wiped a hand across his bare chest and showed her the fingers smeared with white grains. He stood over her till she had taken six of the tablets. 'What about your malaria pills? Have you taken them?'

She shook her head. 'Not today.'

He got the bottle and gave her two tablets, taking one himself. 'You need a nursemaid, Ruth Carter.'

'I feel better already.'

'Good. Let's rustle up some grub. We've got a busy afternoon ahead of us.'

While Ruth put together a snack lunch Smith got to work repairing the mesh screens on the doors and windows. When the food came he ate and drank as he worked. As Ruth watched him she wondered again at his energy. But Smith was just being practical. He wanted the accommodation free of mosquitoes and flies so they could sleep undisturbed at night. They were going to need every ounce of energy they could muster if his plan was to have any hope of success. He had no doubt about his own strength. But that would not be enough. He needed Ruth. His plan looked possible on paper but he had not mentioned that it could take a full week to shift *Mermaid* across that half mile of jungle and swamp to the creek. Seven days working from dawn to dusk in the heat and humidity of the swamps would sap a giant's strength. He knew he would have to watch over her all the time, making her rest, making her eat and drink at the right times, protecting her, preserving her. It was an odd, almost forgotten experience, being responsible for another human being. It was a cruel coincidence that

125

the only other object of Smith's special care would, as soon as the boat was spotted, be planning his death. But it was not that thought that kept surfacing in his mind as he munched the food and cut and tacked the wire mesh. Rather it was his dependence on Ruth. Needing someone else to help him survive was something he had avoided for a very long time. As the thought nagged him he realised that the last time he had been so dependent was when the boy Blik had hauled him out of the river and guided him to safety.

He left Ruth to clear up and told her to meet him on the fo'c'slehead when she was ready. By the time she arrived he had an awning rigged over the windlass. He left her there in the shade and climbed down to the ground and went to work near the stern. Ruth watched, trying to make sense of what he was doing with wires and blocks and tackles. She watched him hammering spikes into a great hardwood to make steps, then clambering up and disappearing in the foliage. Back down to the ground and across to the starboard quarter to repeat the process on another tree. After almost an hour very little seemed to have been achieved. Then he started heaving on a tackle and suddenly it all made sense. A wire rose into view, spanning the gap between the two trees. As it came tight, Ruth saw that it ran exactly across *Mermaid's* stern and about thirty feet above the deck. In mid-span it carried a block with a wire runner already rove through it. Smith came back on board and carried the ends of that wire up to the bow. He shackled one end to the runner on the derrick serving the hold and brought the other end up to where Ruth was waiting at the windlass.

He dipped a mug into a bucket of water and drank deeply. He swept the sweat from his face with an arm and grinned at her. 'Now we're almost ready to start.'

'Start what?' she asked.

126

'Shifting the ballast. I did explain that, didn't I?'

'Yes. I was just wondering. What do we do if the ship doesn't tip up like you say she should?'

'Not to worry. I'll cut a few logs and dangle them off the stern. That'll do it.'

She shook her head. 'You've got an answer for everything. You just won't accept defeat.'

He put a hand on her shoulder. 'Ruth, when you run out of answers in this place, you're dead.'

She watched as he started stripping the hatch covers from the hold. The heat was stifling under the awning. The glare of the sun was cut off but the air was hot and humid, motionless. Ruth shivered. Smith's words belied the smile on his lips. They had sounded like a prediction.

It was another half-hour before he came up out of the hold, the sweat dripping off him as if he had just stepped from a shower. 'Hot,' he said as he drank water and swallowed salt tablets. 'Now we're really ready to start. That's the first tray of ballast loaded. I'll show you how this works.' He started the windlass and showed Ruth how to throw turns of wire on to the end drum. 'Watch.' He threw on another turn and took in the wire hand over hand. 'See. It's simple.' The derrick wire came in and the cargo tray rose into view from the hold. He held the wire, letting the drum turn freely inside the coils, and the tray stopped in mid-air. 'Watch.' He threw off two turns of wire and fed it backwards over the moving drum. The tray dropped slowly back down into the hold. 'Easy, isn't it?'

Ruth was not convinced. 'I suppose it's easy if you're a longshoreman.'

'You'll soon be that, Ruth Carter. In the next day or two you're going to learn more about wires and windlasses and anchor chains than most sailors ever do. Here.' He handed her a pair of leather-faced work gloves. 'Use these. They'll be hot but they'll save your hands. You take this drum and

I'll take the other. Just do what I tell you when I tell you. You'll haul up the tray, hold it while I take up the slack on the wire from the span across the stern, then as I take the strain, you slack off. That way we'll be able to put down the ballast just where we want it on the stern.'

Ruth put on the gloves and made a face. It was like putting her hands into ovens.

'Here we go.' He put her hands on the wire and guided them to throw on the turns and heave in. The tray came up with its load of ballast pigs. 'Hold it like that. Good. You're on your own now. You're doing fine.' Smith picked up the slack on the stern wire. 'Now, very easy, slowly. You slack as I heave.'

That first load had a jerky passage aft but Ruth was getting the hang of it by the time the tray landed on the stern. 'What'd I tell you,' said Smith. 'You're a born sailor. Take a rest and top up with water while I stow that lot and load up the tray again.'

It was on the fourth and last load that *Mermaid* tipped her stern down. She had seemed so solid that Smith was not expecting it. He was already silently cursing his luck and wondering how many trees he would have to cut up and hang off the stern to bring her bow up off the ground. She tipped suddenly when the last tray was just aft of midships and still held on tight wires from the derrick and the stern span. The bow rising up threw Ruth off balance. Her wire ran slack and the tray crashed on to the deckhouse, sliding aft and spilling pig iron over on to the deck and out into the scuppers. Smith swore and let his own wire go slack. He ran round and stopped the windlass.

'I'm sorry. I made a mess of that, Smithy.'

'Doesn't matter. She's tipped. You take a breather. I'll clear up that lot down aft.'

Ruth leaned on the bulwark, sipping from the mug, hoping for a breath of air. She flexed her fingers to ease the

128

stiffness from working with the wire and the puckering of the skin from the wet heat of the gloves. Out astern, through the tops of the trees, she could see the mountain, its snow band mocking her sweat-blackened shirt and slacks. There did seem to be some air now. The sun was in the west, lowering fast, already shielded by the trees. She thought it was a swarm of insects at first, buzz, buzz, buzz. Then it was obviously the sound of a plane. She remembered the helicopter. It broke suddenly from over the trees, low. The downdraught from the rotors flapped the awning and she shouted with joy as the air buffeted her body. The plane went away but turned and came in over *Mermaid*, bow to stern, slowed down, inspecting.

Smith was standing up at the stern, waving. The plane accelerated away, gaining height, going back towards the river into the setting sun. The engine noise faded and the small jungle sounds came back. Ruth lost her elation. Smith had been right. The plane had searched out the boat, looked it over and gone away. She watched him coming back along the deck, up under the awning, beside her, taking the mug from her hand, dipping it into the bucket and drinking. 'Why?' she asked.

'The chopper?'

'Yes. It did just what you said it would. Found us then went away. Why?'

He emptied the mug. 'It's a long story, Ruth. I'll tell you what. Let's use the last of the light to haul these logs I cut this morning in under the bow. Then we'll call it a day and I'll tell you about President Blik and me.'

Chapter 9

'We met a long time ago, Blik and me. During the war.'
Smith shook the tall glass, making the ice cubes clink,
watching them dip and bob and swirl. He took a long drink
of the well-watered whisky. They were in the saloon. It
seemed cool, almost cold, with the sun gone and the sudden
darkness outside. The overhead fans breezed down on
them. 'I was running from the Japs. I fell into the river,
up in the gorges. I'd probably have drowned if Blik hadn't
been there. He was fishing. I was the biggest fish he'd ever
caught.' Smith smiled at the memory. 'He was just a boy.
Ten. Very formal manners. I remember him standing there
and looking down at me and bowing and introducing himself. He's half-caste, y'know. Dutch father, Javanese mother.
He was an orphan by then, living in the bush with some
of the workers from his old man's plantation. He took me
back to them and they contacted my little private army.
Pogostick was one of my crew then. They came and collected me and we went back to war. Blik came with us.'

'I remember reading somewhere about his exploits during
the war,' said Ruth. 'It all seemed pretty fantastic for a
youngster. But I never realised he was only ten years old.'

Smith grinned and sipped his drink. 'That version isn't
quite accurate. You might say that the facts were bent in
the interests of better public relations. Don't ever say it out
loud but the truth is that he was a sort of mascot. Useful
too. He was quite a good wee scout. Even better cook boy.
But the only thing he ever stuck a knife into was a wild
pig; a dead wild pig. Not that his stories aren't true. He
was there. He saw it all. He just didn't do any of it.'

'You?'

'And Pogostick. And the others. We kept ourselves busy. Towards the end we got tired of just watching and sending radio reports. We turned quite nasty. The headhunters got to like Jap. Said it had more flavour than European.'

Ruth grimaced. 'That was some background for a growing boy.'

'Name me a nice war?' asked Smith. He took a drink. 'Anyway, Blik stayed with me till the end. There was nowhere for him to go so I took him back to Port Bancourt. He had to go to school. He didn't like that but we had evenings and week-ends and holidays together. He helped me build *Mermaid*. We were good pals.'

'So you're like a stepfather to him?'

'Sort of.'

Ruth shook her head. 'It's amazing. How do you feel about your adopted son being president of his country?'

'Certainly not overcome. After all, it was me who put him there.'

She laughed. 'Come off it, Smithy. Who's bending the facts now? Even I know about President Blik's bloodless revolution. Are you saying you organised that too?'

'That's right.' He drained his glass and refilled it. 'You don't believe me, do you? Well, try this on for size.' He sipped his fresh drink and put the glass down on the table. 'By the time I'd refitted *Mermaid* just enough to start trading her round the coast and up the Paradise, Blik was starting senior school. He'd done enough by then to show he had plenty brains so, since I wasn't going to be there in Port Bancourt all the time, I sent him to boarding school in Australia. It was like that saying about absence making the heart grow fonder. We became really close. We wrote to each other every week. He came back here for holidays. It wasn't really like father and son. More like brothers. I knew him better than anyone else in the world. I suppose it was the same for him, with me. Anyway, to cut a long story short, when he finished school in Australia, he went to university in the States, then on to Paris for a couple of years. He finished there in, let's see, yes, 1958.' Smith took a drink. 'Out here, the Indonesians were stirring things up. Sukarno was in power then. He was pushing the British in Borneo, he was pushing the Dutch wherever he could find them. He had his eyes firmly fixed on Dutch New Guinea and he wasn't ignoring this island. After New Guinea, this would be the only Dutch toehold in the Pacific. Blik was like a gift from the gods to the Indonesians. They noticed him in Paris. They wooed him and they won him. I've always rather liked them since then. They brought Blik back to me. If it hadn't been for them he'd still've been in Europe or the States. That's where he's really at home.' Smith scratched his chin. 'Where was I? Oh, yes. Well, he didn't arrive back here overnight. They took their time preparing him. He came back in '61, on holiday, to see me. We came up the Paradise and talked it all through. At least he talked. I just listened. When he went away, I talked to the British and the Dutch.' Smith got to his feet and paced up and down the saloon. 'Try and picture the situation, Ruth. The Dutch had lost heart out here. They'd already decided to give up without any more fight. In '62 Dutch New Guinea was to be abandoned to the Indonesians and become West Irian. The Australians, who run the bigger part of New Guinea, didn't fancy that but couldn't do much about it. Up here the British certainly didn't want an Indonesian province on their western border. So it was agreed, here in this saloon, at this table, that I should arrange for Blik to set up an independent republic when the Dutch left. It appealed to the Dutch sense of humour. They'd taken a lot of stick from Sukarno.'

'How did Blik feel about this plan?'

'He didn't feel anything. He didn't know about it.'

132

'But he is the president. It is a republic. How did you work that?'

'It wasn't too difficult. It's very easy to cheat people who trust you.' Smith sat down and drank some whisky. 'In the end, of course, he came to see that I'd done the right thing. He even accepted that my motives were good. So they were. I set it up with the British and the Dutch but I did it for my own reasons. I wasn't conniving at setting up a puppet régime. I believed Blik would do a good job. I think he has done. I think he's just beginning. But that's jumping the gun.' He pushed aside his glass. 'You asked how I worked it. Well, Blik came back in '62. I'd organised what he's since called his peasant army. I still had my contacts from the war. There was no shooting. Just talk about the brave new world and marching here and there taking over plantations the Dutch had already deserted. Then there was a complication. The Indonesians sent across a company of commandos to put a bit of fire into the revolution. I picked them up off the coast and brought them up the river. I sent Blik on ahead towards the capital. I followed with my men and the commandos. We had a big party the night before we were due to meet up with Blik. When the Indonesians woke up they were neatly trussed like pigs on their way to market. Blik was furious but he didn't take long to get the point. He didn't take long to see that having his own country had special attractions. So he marched triumphantly into the capital at the head of his peasant army, paraded the Indonesians in the main square, made a marvellous speech about not only saving the people from the Dutch imperialists but also saving them from the new Indonesian imperialists. Then the Dutch governer did all the handing over stuff and that was that. A bit Gilbert and Sullivan but everyone was happy.'

'How about the Indonesians?'

'They were shipped back home. Blik was showing him-

133

self to be magnanimous. I doubt if Sukarno was as nice to them.'

Ruth sipped her drink and looked puzzled. 'Smithy, you started to tell me this because of the helicopter. I must have missed the point.'

'No, you haven't missed the point. You haven't heard it yet.' Smith leaned forward in his chair. 'The point is that Blik wasn't in Government House more than a few hours before he discovered that I'd set the whole thing up with the Dutch and the British. He was a bit upset. We talked about it. He was pleased enough about the result. What he couldn't forgive was that I'd deceived him. It was like knocking out one of the main props of his life. He spoke very quietly. No histrionics. He told me that if he ever caught me out again, he'd kill me. He meant it too.'

Ruth nodded slowly. 'I can understand that. His feeling of being let down, I mean. But that's all years ago. I still don't get the point about the helicopter.'

'He thinks he's caught me out again. That chopper was checking up to see if I'd survived the flood. It'll be back every day. It'll chart our progress back to the river. Blik will love every minute of it. He'll know that I know what's happening. He'll enjoy stretching out the agony, knowing that I know I can't escape. He can take me any time he wants. He won't be in a hurry. He's a good hunter. He had a good teacher.'

'You're crazy, Smithy. People don't behave like that. What is it you're supposed to have done?'

'That doesn't matter. It's gone on for a long time. It was going on even before Blik's revolution. But he's got evidence now. He's a man who keeps his word. He's read the wrong meaning into the evidence but it's that kind of evidence. He'll want to know if he can keep his word. You see, Ruth, Blik's never killed anyone in his life. If he can kill me it'll open up a whole new world for him. Not a nice world but one in which ambitious politicians are welcome.'

'So why not deny him the chance?'

'Because he has to make the decision. Anyway, I don't have much choice.' Smith lifted his glass and grinned. 'But I don't kill easily.'

'I'll drink to that,' said Ruth quietly. Then her eyes lit up. 'Smithy, I've got it. I'm your way out. Once he knows I'm on board with you, the president won't dare do anything. Americans may not be the most popular people in the world nowadays but we do have our uses. There's a lot of American money coming in here. With me on board, he'll have to let you get back to Port Bancourt. Then you'll be safe.'

Smith stopped his glass short of his lips. That might be true but it was a hell of a chance to take with Ruth's life. It was all guesswork. It was years since he'd met Blik. But he needed Ruth to help him get *Mermaid* back to the river. That would be safe enough. Blik wouldn't try anything with an American chopper. He smiled to himself. Chopper. How appropriate. 'Maybe you're right,' he told her. 'Welcome aboard, lifesaver. As a small token of my gratitude, I'll let you have a bucket of water to wash in.'

'Marvellous. I'm glad I thought of that.'

'I'll get some dinner ready for us.'

'I won't be long. I'll help.'

'No, Ruth. You take your time. You've worked hard enough already. Anyway I must have one decent meal a day if I'm to keep my strength up.'

She made a face. 'Unfair to Ruth.'

'But true. Let's face it. You're not the best cook in the world.'

She watched him go through to the galley. The smile faded from her face. It was a fantastic story but she knew it was true. She had escaped from her brother's mad world in the valley to the madder world of *Mermaid* and Smith

135

and President Blik. She prayed she would turn out to be a lifesaver.

*   *   *

The president was walking in the garden at Government House. He liked the garden. He liked the house. The Dutch did that kind of thing well. They had chosen the best site, on the hill overlooking the harbour. The house was in the grand manner, all in white stucco, with a colonnaded front, a magnificent entrance hall leading to big reception rooms, and a great staircase running up to the first floor. The grounds were cleverly laid out to give shade at all times of the day and to open up breathtaking views over the town and the harbour. The sun had just set. It would soon be dark. The views would be even better then, the lights etching the shape of the bay and the big island offshore.

But Blik was not thinking of the house or the garden or the views. He was trying to fight off the despair he had felt since the day before. It was the anti-climax he felt when he was hunting, after the kill. But it was more than that. He had seen his quarry but the flood had snatched it from him. Smith was very special game. He deserved a proper death. He had earned his right to that. Now there was no trace of the boat. The search had gone on all day, right down to the estuary and out to sea. Blik had sent Major Loder out again in the afternoon. He had to have proof. He had to know for sure that Smith was dead. Only then would he accept the fact that he could never put himself to the test. He would never know if he could have kept his promise to kill Smith. That was important. Either way that test would have freed him for ever from Smiddy. He had to know what had happened to *Mermaid*.

'Sir.'

Blik looked up and searched out the voice in the half light. 'Yes. Over here.'

'It's me, sir. Loder.'

The president limped towards the major, wincing at the pain in his muscles from the beating he had taken at the cliff the morning before. 'Well? Did you find anything?'

'Mr President, we found the boat.'

'Where?'

'Not away down the river. Out in the jungle, east of the river. That's British territory. I didn't think they'd mind me overflying since it was an errand of mercy.'

'Who would know, out there in the swamps?'

'No one, I guess. Except your friend. He gave us a wave.'

Blik caught his breath. 'Smith? Alive?'

'I don't know if it was your Captain Smith but he was very much alive.'

'You're sure it was *Mermaid*? Must've been. There aren't any other boats on the river. There was enough left to recognise it as some kind of ship?'

'It's all left. Don't ask me how it survived that flood but it's sitting up there right in the middle of a clutch of trees just like it was in dry dock. It's a bit beat up, funnel's gone, that kind of thing, but it's certainly not all in bits. Your friend's got a lot of luck working for him, Mr President.'

'Major, if Smith fell into a Paris sewer he'd come up smelling of Chanel Number 5. But it's not all luck. He's been surviving for a very long time. It's almost a profession with him.'

'Well, he's going to need some help this time. Will I lift him out of there in the morning, sir?'

'Certainly not. Leave him alone.'

'But, sir, you don't understand. He's bang in the middle of that swamp. Are you going to let him try and walk out?'

'He won't come out without his ship, Major.'

'Then he won't come out, not ever. There's no water. Just puddles here and there. He's high and dry and miles from the river.'

Blik put a hand on Loder's shoulder. 'It's going to be an interesting assignment for you, Major. You fly a check on Smith every day from now on. Keep me in touch. He'll surprise you, I promise.'

'Whatever you say, sir.' He turned away.

'Oh, Major. Fly that check from a safe distance. Captain Smith has an uncertain temper. He's the best shot there is in these parts.'

'Thank you, sir. I'll remember that.' He swore to himself. Soft number, that's what they called this. Like in a madhouse.

Blik could smell the blossom all around, he could see the view of the bay in the darkness, he could feel the evening breeze on his face. He smiled in anticipation of the hunt.

Chapter 10

Smith was up an hour before dawn. He made coffee and called Ruth. They were at work by sun-up, Smith down on the ground, Ruth at the windlass in the bows. It took four hours to lay out the line of logs ahead of *Mermaid*, a dozen of them, spaced about fifteen feet apart, looking like a giant railroad in the making, sleepers laid and awaiting the rails. Smith had scouted the first run of ground the day before. He knew that nothing was going to be as simple as it had looked on paper. The ground was fairly flat but criss-crossed with a maze of little channels cut by the swamp water. The logs had to lie over solid ground. Not that it was very solid, still soaked by the recent flood. He placed his blocks, stropped each log, shackled on the wires running back on board and bellowed instructions through a megaphone. Ruth had learned her lessons well the day before. The windlass drums turned, the wire tightened, the logs rolled into place one by one. Smith watched them flattening the tangle of bush and creeper. That was good. That mat of vegetation would stiffen up the waterlogged earth.

With the logs in place he told Ruth to take a breather while he hacked his way across the swamp to lay the blocks for the wires to haul the anchors and cables out ahead of the boat. He had picked two trees about a thousand feet ahead to lash the blocks to. He had nine hundred feet of chain on each anchor. With the dog-leg course dictated by the ground and the available trees for hauling out the anchors he guessed it would take at least five flights of cable to move *Mermaid* the half mile to the creek. He wondered if maybe he was being optimistic in guessing at a week for the

139

trip. The first move would be the real test. If the boat moved on her makeshift rollers and neither slipped off sideways nor drove them into the ground with her weight, then he would know that his plan might succeed. With luck there would be no more tree felling. As the boat moved forward, he would stop her every couple of hundred feet, fix blocks to the tight chains, run wires aft and drag out ahead the logs the boat had left astern. The softness of the ground was his biggest worry. Even if there was a tendency for the stern to slip sideways that could be controlled by wires led out on either beam. His swinging machete beat the tempo of the theme that filled his head. Back to the river. Back to the Paradise.

Ruth watched him till he was small in the distance, sometimes out of sight behind the swamp grass and bush. She leaned on the bulwark and stared at the line of logs. It was all starting to happen just the way he had said. What a man. She looked down and caught sight of the figurehead. She realised it was only the second time she had seen it. There was the mane of bronze hair and the arms flung back as if in flight. There was the scar where the right breast had been severed. She put a hand on her own breast. One difference, thank goodness. The mermaid intrigued her. She wanted to see it properly. She checked ahead. Smith would not need her for some time yet. She climbed down to the ground and went round to the bow and stared up at the figurehead. It had taken a beating. It was scratched and scarred. One fluke of the tail was missing. But the likeness was astonishing. She changed her position. The likeness stayed, even grew. It was not Ruth but it was Ruth in essence. The hair, the small ears, the widespread eyes, the line of the nose and jaw, the big mouth, the proud set of the head on the long neck. Even the shape of a hand, its fingers trailing gracefully under the flare of the bow. Ruth shut her eyes and told herself to stop being a fool. She told herself she was

140

imagining it all. It had started with Smith and now she was making it come true because she wanted to believe in the outrageous coincidence. Maybe she wanted to believe that there was no coincidence, that it had been predestined, that it all meant something. She opened her eyes. Nothing had changed. Nothing but how she felt. With her eyes open, the choice between destiny and coincidence seemed irrelevant. What mattered was the feeling that she had come home. Not to a home that was a place, rather a home that was a feeling. It was a warm, contented feeling but exciting, full of promise. It was a quite different home from her parents' home, or the home she might have had with Max Haltone, or Harry the Hippie or anyone other than Smith. She knew it was a dream home, impossible, unattainable. She knew that maybe that was why she wanted it so much. She was happy and sad, resigned but filled with hope. She picked her way through the undergrowth back to the ladder and started climbing on board.

Half-way up the ladder she turned her head and saw the flowers. Just one patch, a little riot of colour in the dense greens and browns of the trees and the bush. She climbed back down and went over and plucked the flowers. It seemed a shame to pull them but she wanted them for the saloon table. She found some jungle fern and took a few stalks of the tall swamp grass, green shading to brown. She held out the completed bunch. Gorgeous. She put her face down among the blossoms. Their coolness reminded her of the heat. The delicate scents dispelled for a moment the stench of the swamp. She turned back to the boat, hugging the flowers to her.

The way back took her close under *Mermaid*'s stern. The splash of colour caught her eye then was gone. She stepped backwards, thinking it was a solitary brilliant flower to add to her collection. She found the spot. The colour was shining up through the creeper, reddish yellow round a dazzling centre like a spot of light. She laid down her flowers and parted the creeper with her hands. She smiled. Ever been had? It was one of the ballast bars they had shifted yesterday. She looked up. The spot where she was was directly under one of the boat's stern fairleads. The bar must have skidded through and overboard when that last tray spilled. She was puzzled by the light she had seen. The bar was grey all round except for the flat top which was a reddish yellow. Iron was greyish so the top must be one of these paints they use on ships. Why paint one side of a piece of pig iron? She bent down to lift the bar. She could hardly move it. She frowned. Was pig iron that heavy? Something was sticking to her fingers, a grey flake, like old paint. So the grey was paint. She knelt down and peered at the top. The colour was not paint but a natural sheen. Then she saw the light source again. It was not on the surface but indented into it. The sun's rays, slanting in under the counter dazzled her as they reflected up out of the gouge. Bright. Like gold.

'Gold is the heaviest metal. Gold is almost twice as heavy as lead which is half as heavy again as iron.' A teacher's voice came back over a dozen years. Another voice, Manutami's, wise man of the Pochaks. Tears of the sun. White men. Death. Dead bodies sealed up with tears of the sun. Forbidden land. Not a voice, a picture. Ruth standing on the Pochaks' forbidden land looking across the river at their forbidden cliff; Smith rising dripping from the river. Smith's voice last night. 'Blik thinks he's caught me out again. It doesn't matter what I'm supposed to have done. It's gone on for a long time.'

Ruth crouched on the ground staring at the ballast bar but not seeing it. Instead she saw a desert where seconds before there had been flowers and fountains. She heard Smith's voice but she heard it as the snarling of the reptiles crawling on her barren wilderness.

Smith swore. Where the hell's she got to? To his waist he was layered in mud and slime. Sweat ran in rivers down his face and back and chest. He took a long swallow from his water bottle. 'Ruth, where the hell are you? We haven't got all bloody day, y'know.' He was under the bow with the messenger rope he had dragged back from where he had set the blocks. That messenger would heave out the wires that would heave out the anchors that would heave *Mermaid* out of the swamp. He swore again and dropped the rope. He went along to the ladder to climb up and rouse Ruth from whatever she was doing. He saw her as he reached the ladder. 'Oh, there you are. Come on. We've got work to do.' She seemed not to hear him. He went towards her. 'Wakey, wakey. Work.' He saw the flowers. Christ. Women. 'Very thoughtful, I'm sure. Can we fit some work in between the homely touches, d'you think?' No reaction. She was unnaturally still, like stone. 'Ruth, are you all right? What's the matter? Are you ill? Something bite you?' He searched around. Nothing. He stepped closer and saw the ballast bar. He saw the scraped surface and the deep scratch. His eyes flicked up to the boat's stern. He did not recognise her voice, flat, empty.

'It is gold, isn't it?'

'Yes, it's gold.'

'All of it?'

'Yes.'

She got slowly to her feet and faced him. He was shocked at the change in her. She seemed crushed. She spoke quietly, uncertainly at first. 'You bastard.' Her rage put venom into her voice. 'You rotten, lying, thieving bastard. No wonder Blik wants to kill you. I hope he does. D'you hear me? I hope he does.' She was screaming at him and close to tears.

'It's not like that, Ruth. I'd better tell you the story.'

'Don't bother. I don't want to hear it. You've got a story

for everything. You've got one for Blik, and one for why you hide yourself away from the world, and one for your high principles and one for . . . for . . . Bastard. You're a bastard, Smith.' She pushed past him, her foot catching the bunch of flowers and scattering them.

'I said it wasn't like that.' His voice was angry now. 'You're going to hear that story whether you want to or not.'

'Bastard.'

He ran after her and caught her arm and swung her round. 'I've had enough of you, Ruth Carter. It's about time you came down off that mountain of yours. That mountain that stuffs your ears and stitches up your eyes.' He held her as she struggled. 'You're one to talk about hiding from the world. You and your two years with the Pochaks and your nutty brother, you with your breathless little-girl-lost bit then the big tease and the arch looks and the I've-found-my-father-figure smirk and all the time you'd run a mile at the sound of an unzipped fly. You need a good fright, girlie, and I'm just the man to give you that.'

She hacked his shins and broke free. He went after her and caught her with a flying tackle. They crashed to the ground and rolled over, grappling, fighting. He turned her on to her back and locked her arms. He twined his legs round hers and let his weight press down on her. She turned her head and sank her teeth into his hand. The pain leapt up his arm and stunned him. He reached round with his other hand and grabbed her hair. He pulled on it till her teeth came out of his hand. She arched her body and twisted and they rolled over and over on the floor of the jungle, splashing in and out of puddles of mud and slime. All the time she was screaming abuse. Suddenly his mouth was over hers and the curses were stifled. Pain exploded again in his head as her teeth clamped on his lower lip. He could taste the blood. He flexed his arms and legs to hold her still and crushed his body down on her. He could feel her breasts heaving against his chest. The pain in his mouth was excruciating but he made no attempt to free himself. Instead he pressed his face closer into hers. Then it all changed. His lip was freed and her tongue was in his mouth. Her arms and legs and body still struggled, but not against, with. Oh Christ. He freed himself and rolled away from her. He got to his feet. There was blood on his hand and blood in his mouth. He spat it out.

Ruth lay on the ground, staring up at him, confused, puzzled.

He stretched out a hand. 'I'm sorry about that. I apologise.'

She waited till she had her breath back then sat up, took the offered hand and let herself be pulled to her feet. She said nothing, just stood there then hit him with her right hand. The slap echoed round the clearing. Before his focus was back she hit him with her other hand, then again with the right one.

He shook his head. She had the right kind of muscles to help him get back to the river.

'I . . .I . . .'

'Don't say a word, Miss Carter. I may be a bastard but I'm not a stupid bastard.'

She gave him a tiny, tired smile.

'Can I tell you about the gold now?' he asked.

She shrugged. 'If you must.'

'Maybe I've kept it to myself too long. Over here.'

They sat down on the end of one of the logs lying under the boat. They were on the side away from the sun. It was hot and humid but the shade gave some relief.

'It all began on my first trip up the Paradise after the war. But it really began before that, when I fell into the river and Blik hauled me out. I didn't just fall into the river. I was hiding out from the Japs in a hole in the top of that cliff. When I slipped I thought I was dead but I dropped into water and ended up in the river. On my first trip with *Mermaid* I found I couldn't take her into the gorges so I left her at anchor and went up through the gorges on foot. I've often wondered why it was I felt I had to go back up there. I was curious about how I'd got into the river but I knew what I'd find. There had to be an underwater passage between the river and that shaft in the cliff. I wasn't even sure if it would still be there. The ground round the mountain's pretty unstable. The passage might have closed up long ago. Maybe it was just nostalgia. Blik and I had met in the gorges. By then he was away to school and I'd lost my pal. Anyway, whatever the reasons, I went up and found my cliff. It only took me two or three dives to find the way in. Then I found the gold. At first I found the skeletons. Oh yes, the Pochaks' story's true. There's some armour and weapons. They were Spaniards all right. All laid out like fish on a slab. I remembered Pogostick telling me the story of the forbidden land. They were really scared of that place. Still are, as you know. During the war they wouldn't even cross it to escape the chase.'

Smith wiped at the sweat on his face and neck. 'The gold was in a little chamber off the main shaft. It didn't take me long to realise what I'd found. These bars are very heavy, too heavy. They're only roughly regular in shape. The Spaniards apparently didn't have any means of melting down what the Pochaks brought them. They must have used some sort of big hammer, maybe a suspended stone, to beat all the little bits together in some sort of mould. That's one of the odd things about gold in its pure state. It's the only metal that welds itself under pressure. Put two pieces of pure gold together and hammer them, and they become one piece of gold. But that's not really part of the story though it turned out to be handy that it was all in sort of bars. Anyway, I remember sitting in that cave trying to come to terms with knowing that I had more wealth than I could really understand, if only I could get it out of there. It was such a fortune that, for the time being, I forgot all about my disenchantment with money and the world it bought. I never doubted I could sell it. I knew from my work in war surplus that ways could always be found of getting a wanted item to a willing buyer. I never wondered then what I could do with all that money. It was a huge treasure and I'd found it and it seemed natural to turn it into cash. I knew I could do nothing then. The boat was miles away and the river up through the gorges was unnavigable. So I dived out of the cliff and headed back for *Mermaid*. I went slowly, testing depths, checking obstructions, making notes and charts. By the time I got back on board I knew what I had to do. Back to Port Bancourt, load up with explosives, up the Paradise again and blast a channel up through the gorges. If I could open a way through to that cliff, I could clean out the whole hoard in one trip.

'Well, I blasted my way up to that cliff with *Mermaid*. Then something happened that changed everything. I didn't realise that at first. I was just furious at my plans going wrong. I'd got just three bars on board when the rain started. Not just the usual island downpour. A look at the glass and a look at the sky told me the whole story. It happens every two or three years. A typhoon bends nearer the island than usual and the rain comes down in buckets for anything up to a week. You get flash floods in all the mountain streams and then the Paradise overflows across these swamps here. Even that fortune in the cliff didn't keep me up there. I cut and ran. I made it out of the gorges and then I kept going till I was clear of the river. It was a month before I came back. By then I'd thought it all through. I knew I neither needed nor wanted the money.

But I did want the challenge of regularly taking *Mermaid* up through the gorges. And I wanted the fun of piling up a fortune in gold in the bottom of my boat and using it for the same purpose that I'd been using the iron ballast. It started with the problem of what to do with these first three bars. I didn't want some nosey customs man finding them. So I gave them a coat of paint and stowed them with the pig iron in the hold. They just disappeared. So from then on I replaced the iron ballast with gold ballast. It's all gold now but that took me all of twenty-five years. Just a few bars each trip. Twenty-five years of beating these gorges and that underwater passage.' Smith grinned. 'And for what? For nothing except the achievement. A wee allegory of life, Ruth. Self imposed challenges taken on and beaten; and so much energy used in the achieving that that becomes the object rather than the means. Did I have an object? I don't know. But that treasure in my bilges has taught me a lot and it's made me laugh a lot. It taught me first about values. It taught me that all our values are illusions. D'you know how much that gold's worth?'

She shook her head.

'At the pegged rate about thirteen and a half million but on the free market not less than fifteen million.'

'Fifteen million what?' she asked.

'Dollars.'

'American dollars?'

'That's right.'

'Wow.'

'It's a lot of money, isn't it? But of course it's not worth that to me, not on board *Mermaid*. There it's worth whatever it costs me to replace it with eleven tons of iron ballast.' Smith smiled as she tried to work that out. 'It's no more worth fifteen million dollars than a hundred square inches of painting done a few centuries ago is worth five or six million. Both things have their ridiculous price justified by unique quality and shortage of supply. And that price is justified for anyone who must have these unique qualities. But if you don't need these qualities the things have little or no value. So my gold's worth almost nothing. Except in what it does for me.' Smith chuckled then winced at the pain in his wounded mouth. 'It's done a lot for me. It's been the secret knowledge that everyone has who can stand back and laugh at the world. Like the artist who knows he's right, like the aristocrat who can trace his family back a thousand years, like the drop-out who needs nothing that others feel essential. In my case, maybe more like that man who confused people by always grinning at them. It didn't matter what they did or said, he always grinned. He even managed to grin when his family was gathered round his death bed. His was a simple trick. When he looked at people he always imagined them with no clothes on.' Smith watched Ruth and saw her puzzled frown softening. 'That's right. You're getting the idea. The world's geared to people with clothes on. Clothes maketh the man, even more they maketh the woman. When everyone's stark naked, society changes. The nude general, the nude politician, the nude actor, the nude tycoon, the nude priest, yes, even the nude mannequin, maybe her even more so, they all lose their ability to impress. In the nude society the only ones who get away with it are the kids under three. That's what my gold did for me. It stripped the world to the buff. I had the means to buy and sell almost anyone but they didn't know that so they went on looking at me and everyone else as if what they were seeing with their eyes was real.'

He stared at an insect crawling on the creeper between his feet. 'Of course, that's just the plus side. There's always a minus side too. My minus side started to show when the gold in the cliff started to run out. I was forced to start looking at what I was doing and why I was doing it. That's rough when you've spent your life laughing at other people. To sit down and face the fact that your big joke is as stupid and senseless as the serious things other people do, that's quite an exercise. You see, Ruth, I had to start thinking about what to do when there was no more gold left in that cliff. Last trip there were only two bars. That should've been the last trip. But I only took one. That gave me a few more weeks to try and find an answer. By this trip I still didn't know the answer. I even thought maybe I should take the last bar and next trip start putting the gold back into the cliff. But you and the mountain fixed all that.' He saw her head lift. 'Yes, you. The mountain first because when I dived the other morning I found the passage blocked. There was one bar of gold left and I couldn't reach it. Maybe I could have reached it by going round and up to the top of the cliff and trying to find the way in from there. But you arrived and that was out. Then when we anchored and you told me about your professor friend, I felt I was getting near to the answer. I knew that Blik would pick up the clues. I knew how he'd react. What's happened so far has proved I was right. But it hasn't got anything to do with finding an answer to my problem. It might solve one problem, a problem I've tried to pretend didn't exist. You see, I've made a fetish out of being my own man. Blik's the only person I've ever felt close to. He's the only person I've tried to guide the way a parent would guide a child. In a way that stopped about eight years ago. But he was a man by then so I'm still intrigued to know if I gave him enough to let him trust me. I'll soon know. If he does kill me I'll have failed but if I die quickly enough I won't even have time to realise it. If he doesn't kill me, I'll know I've succeeded but then I'll still have to live with my real problem. What do you do when your bilges are stuffed with fifteen million dollars' worth of gold?'

It was a moment or two before Ruth realised he was asking a question. 'What do you do? If you don't want it, if you can't use it, give it away. Surely the world's full enough of deserving causes.'

Smith shook his head. 'It's not as easy as that. What's a deserving cause? Giving it away might cause more problems than keeping it as ballast. At least I know it's doing a useful job where it is.'

'Why not just fling it away? Drop it in this swamp. Let it sink into the mud and be lost for ever.'

'What would that prove? That's just pretending the problem doesn't exist. There must be some way I can use that gold to good purpose. I can't imagine what it is but I know I'll recognise it when it comes along.'

'Smithy, don't you realise you're setting yourself impossible conditions. You're setting things up so there won't ever be a solution. You don't want a solution. You're in love with your crazy problem.'

'Maybe I am. But that's the way I live. I set myself impossible tasks and I find ways to make them possible. When I find that I've set myself a task I can't crack, then I won't be very interested in going on living. Don't shake your head, Ruth. I'm not as resigned as all that. I'm still hale and hearty and just as devious as most human beings. Maybe more so. When I find the one I can't crack, I'll probably get round it by thinking up something even more impossible that needs tackling. Then I'll convince myself that it's more important than the one I couldn't solve.' He sat up straight and turned his head. 'Our chopper's early today.' The noise of the plane grew quickly. Smith got up and walked out into the clearing. He watched the plane as it circled twice in a wide sweep, staying out of rifleshot.

He waited till it broke off and headed back for the capital. He walked back by the stern, stooping and collecting Ruth's scattered flowers. She was still sitting on the log, sunk in thought. 'Cheer up,' he told her. 'It's my problem. It'll get solved.' He held out the flowers. 'I'm sorry about roughing you up.' He pressed a hand to his aching mouth.

She looked up. 'Are you?' She took the flowers in her hands and smiled slowly. 'I'm not.'

Chapter 11

It was late in the afternoon before the anchors were in position. There was only an hour of daylight left but Smith was determined to move *Mermaid* before the sun went in. Even a few feet would mean that the long half-mile journey had begun. These few feet would also prove if there was any real chance of reaching the river.

Ruth listened as Smith explained about heaving on the anchor cables. The windlass was already like an old friend. All through the afternoon she had handled the wires that dragged out the anchors and their chain, pulling the wire off the turning drum, slipping the brake to let the chain rattle out in carefully controlled little runs, watching Smith's hand signals from the ground ahead, listening to and obeying his orders bellowed back through the megaphone, stopping the wire and the chain when it snagged in the bush, waiting while Smith hacked it free, then hauling in again, brake off, brake on, watching, listening.

She was dazed with the heat and the effort. Her eyes, her ears, her reflexes were sharp and exact but they seemed separate from her body, muscles tight and tired, skin puddled in sweat and prickling with extruded salt. Separate too from that part of her brain which kept throwing up a confusion of things seen and feelings felt. Jethro walking down into the Pochak valley, the sky full of birds, a gold bar winking up at her, a table of marvellous food, a church in flames, Smith at the wheel, an avalanche of muddy water, a huge bed, a terrifying forest, a bath of steaming scented water, the sky full of helicopters, Smith lying drunk at her feet, a cloud of rust rising from the rattling windlass

153

gypsy, a furnace, the snow band on the mountain, the feel of Smith's mouth over hers, a wilderness.

'Let's give it a try,' said Smith. The gypsies were in gear. He started the windlass and took up his position in the bows.

Ruth watched the links of the two chains coming in over the windlass. She watched Smith, his hands held out, making circles in the air, conducting the overture to his survival symphony. Stop. Port side out of gear. Heave on starboard. Stop. Port side back in gear. Heave together. Slowly. Slowly. Stop both.

'That looks about right,' he called. 'Watch out for when the weight comes on. The bow's still up in the air. It'll come down with a bit of a bang. Don't worry. Just watch my hands.'

His hands circled, the windlass turned, the chains clanked. The windlass slowed. The weight was coming on. Smith called for more power. Ruth opened the throttle. Clink, clank, clink. Then the bow came down. It hit the logs hard and the boat shuddered from end to end. The windlass raced as it picked up the slack chain. The dropping bow threw Ruth against the windlass, her face close to the clanking chain. She pushed herself up and watched Smith. Her hand found the throttle again. Slow it down. Not too much. Keep it moving. Easy does it. Slow and steady. Her eyes were on Smith's hands but there was something new on the edge of her vision. She looked quickly left. The trees were moving. Crazy. Trees don't move. Of course. The boat's moving. *Mermaid*'s moving. 'Smithy, it's working. We're moving. We're moving.' Her voice was shrill with excitement.

He looked round, his head nodding, his face split with a huge grin. The thumbs on his circling hands were up.

'We're moving. We're moving.' She shouted the words over and over again as *Mermaid* rolled and bumped and skidded across the logs. 'We're moving. We're moving.' She made the words sound like cheers. There were to be no more cheers for the next six days.

Six days of back-breaking work. Six days of sweat. Six days of worry as logs were swallowed up by the swamp, as wires snagged and broke, as *Mermaid*'s stern slipped and slithered out of control. Six days of hand signals and shouted orders. Six days that stretched on through to each night as Smith worked on the engines and straightened the damaged propeller shaft and beat out the dents in the funnel and renewed the rigging. He seemed tireless, driven to a frenzy of effort, filling each waking moment with work to get his boat back to the Paradise, back to the river with everything repaired or replaced, the boat as efficient and spotless as before the lake emptied itself down the mountain. Ruth wondered if he meant to paint *Mermaid* to cover all her scars, maybe even re-gild and colour the figurehead. There was a crazy dedication about it all, like a French aristocrat preening himself in the tumbril as it rumbled towards the guillotine. Six days of growing accustomed to each other, knowing without words being spoken what to do and when to do it. Six days concerned only with each minute as it passed, with no word of what had happened or what might happen. Six days with, each afternoon, the helicopter circling like a patient vulture. Six days with each of them thinking their own thoughts and respecting the other's silence.

Until that sixth day when *Mermaid* sat on the bank of the creek and the helicopter had come and circled and gone, and Smith announced that the gold had to go back into the main hold.

Ruth knew the answer before she asked the question but she had to have her say. 'Smithy, must we move it? Let's just dump it in the creek. It's not a treasure. It's not even ballast. It's a prison. It's a prison you've been in for twenty-five years. Dump it. Break out. Try a bit of freedom.'

'Very eloquent.' He went on fixing the block and tackle to the stern davit. 'It may look like a prison to you. To me it still looks like ballast. Without that ballast *Mermaid* won't trim right for the river. Specially now with what that flood may've done to the channels in the estuary.' He swung the davit over the lazaret hatch. 'I know you mean well, Ruth, but this is one I have to work out for myself.' He opened the hatch. 'Now, are you going to help or do I have a mutiny on my hands?'

*   *   *

Blik was in his office. It had been a frustrating week. There was plenty of paperwork but he had found it difficult to concentrate. His days had been spent putting in time till Loder reported in the afternoons. In the evenings he had savoured *Mermaid*'s progress; he had worried when she seemed to be in difficulties, guessed at how much longer he must wait. He had managed always to be unavailable when Max Haltone made his daily pilgrimage to ask for permission to start on his expedition to the Pochak valley. Mr Soong was keeping the professor at bay. Or had been till that morning. There had been a call for the president. Just to clear up a misunderstanding. It seemed that an American citizen was having some difficulty in getting the necessary papers and assistance to conduct historical research on the island. Maybe it was just an administrative error. There wasn't any special problem, was there? No, of course not, at least not about the professor. Charming chap. Friend of a friend. But there was a problem about the area he wanted to go to. It was on the mountain and the mountain was still in a dangerous state, damage from the flood was extensive, the republic's resources were at full stretch and, as was well known, it was the president's policy only to allow expeditions to areas where the local tribes had been told of the plans and had agreed to them. In all the circumstances this would take some time but the matter did have a high priority. Maybe the professor could be advised to be patient. The president was giving this his personal attention.

The intercom buzzed on his desk.

'Yes?'

'Major Loder is here, sir.'

'Send him in.' Blik got to his feet and licked his lips. 'Major, do come in. You're a little later than usual. No problems, I hope. How is my good friend Captain Smith today?'

'He seems well enough, Mr President. I still can't believe it but I've got to believe what I see. He's made it.'

'The boat's back in the river?' Blik had a moment of panic. Have I misjudged my timing? Have I given him a chance to get away?

'As good as,' said Loder. 'Not in the water yet but on the bank at the end of that creek he's been heading for. After what he's done, the rest's as nothing.'

Blik smiled. 'I did tell you, didn't I? Captain Smith is one of the great survivors.'

'Yes, you told me, sir.' Loder shifted his stance. He wanted to ask Blik what he intended doing now. For a week he had flown watch on that boat as it rolled unbelievably across the swamp. He had tried to imagine what kind of man this Smith must be to take on something like that singlehanded and succeed. The major had a soldier's admiration for guts and resourcefulness. Every day he had listened to Blik on Smith. He would have thought they were friends, that the president was only interested in Smith's safe return to the river, if only he could have forgotten Blik's voice screaming in his headset when the flood started. 'There'll be another pile of photos, Mr

157

President. The lab'll send them up when they're ready.'

'Yes, yes. Soong will look after them. I prefer your word pictures, Major. Much better than any photographs. I feel as if I've been there, helping to move that little ship back towards the river.'

'Yes, sir. If that's all, I'll be off. I'll report as usual tomorrow. I suppose that'll be the end of it.'

'You've done very well, Major. I think we'll call a halt now. You deserve a few days' leave. Put your feet up. Take it easy. Your excellent sergeant too.' He walked over to the window and stared down at the harbour.

'Whatever you say, Mr President.'

Blik's eyes were on the gunboat, his whole little navy. 'I think I'll take a few days off myself. Yes, I think I'll go and shoot a couple of these salt water crocodiles. It's good sport. Has tourist possibilities.'

'I hope you have better luck than last time, sir.'

'Last time?'

'Last week, when I flew you out to shoot pigs.'

The president looked round. He was smiling. 'Thank you, Major. Thank you. Maybe this time I'll get a pig as a bonus.'

Chapter 12

Mermaid took the water next morning. They stood together in the bows as the windlass turned and heaved in the anchor cables link by link. One moment the boat was squatting on the bank, the next the bow sagged as it was hauled out over the water and a log rolled free down and into the creek. It was sudden after that, as if the boat was eager to plunge back into her natural element. She dived down the bank and dug her bows into the water. It spurted up the hawse holes and splashed over the bulwark, wetting Smith and Ruth as they shouted congratulations at each other. The bow lifted and stretched out down the creek as the stern hit the water and threw up a wave over both banks.

'D'you feel it?' shouted Smith. 'D'you feel the change?' He pointed down. 'In your feet. D'you feel it? She's alive again.'

Ruth nodded excitedly. She was close to tears. It was true. *Mermaid* felt different, alive, eager.

The windlass was chattering as it picked up the slack cables. Smith slowed it, let the way come off the boat, picked up more slack, then stopped the windlass as the boat came to rest. The creek was narrow and the water still. The boat could not turn round or come to any harm. There was work to do.

He had been up at first light and shipped the shafts and the propellers, then checked all the intakes, clearing them of the mud and other debris picked up on the long drag across the swamp. Now he had to check if the hull had sprung any leaks with the battering it had taken in the past week. Then the moment of truth when he would try to start the engines.

He went round with the sounding rod checking bilges and tanks. Everything seemed all right but he would check again later. As he picked his way around the decks, stepping over and round the litter of wires and blocks and ropes, he promised himself to clear everything up when they got out into the river. Then he would start the pumps and wash *Mermaid* down till the stench of the swamp was out of his nostrils.

With the boat launched he found himself starting to think about Blik. It had been easy to push all that to the back of his mind when he was fighting the swamp. Leave it there in the back of your mind, Smithy. You've still got plenty to do. Anyway, it might never happen. Maybe you've just made it all up. Crap. What about that chopper every afternoon? I didn't make that up. I know Blik. He'll be waiting for me down in the estuary. And it won't be to hand me a bunch of roses. So you'll think of something. You always do. You always have done. I'd better think of something good this time. Well, try thinking about these engines. Without them, you won't ever get to the estuary.

He took Ruth with him into the wheelhouse. 'Keep your fingers crossed.' He opened the main fuel valve and set the switches on control board. His eyes checked round. It all looked good. He pressed the starter on the starboard engine. It whined and died. Then again. On the third try the engine coughed but failed to catch. Ruth was standing with her eyes shut and fingers crossed on both her hands. Once more. This time it caught and the exhaust roared in triumph. He let it run for a while then eased the throttle and checked over the side on the quarter. Good. Water was spurting out of the discharge. The cooling system was all right. The port engine started on the third squeeze of the starter button. 'It's our day, Ruth. Well, don't just stand there. I haven't been training you all this past week so you can be a passenger. Let's have these anchors up and get out into running water.'

She jumped to attention. 'Yessir, Captain, sir.'

His smile was sad as he watched her up into the bows, busying herself with the windlass. Won't be the same without her. She won't like going but it's the only way. Anyway, I won't have long enough to get maudlin about it. Blik will see to that. 'Heave away, Mr Mate.'

The boat moved slowly down the creek. With the anchors up and the propellers turning it was an even better feeling than when *Mermaid* dived off the bank into the water. Now she was free, unattached to the land or the creek bed, the engines pulsing like twin heart beats, the whole boat throbbing with new life. The trees and the jungle slipped past and astern. The river came in sight, the water green and brown, moving. Smith took a deep breath and slapped the binnacle with his hand. There it is, my lovely. The Paradise. We made it back. He caught sight of Ruth, her head and shoulders thrust out over the bow. The three of us.

His hands on the wheel felt the tug as the bow pushed out into the river. He opened both throttles to half power and the boat seemed to leap clear of the creek, the surging prow sending back the thrilling sound of water split and heaped into a bow wave then gurgling and hissing as it passed along the hull to join the creaming wake astern. Smith's eyes searched the river and the banks. A lot of his landmarks had gone with the flood. He picked a spot well out in the stream where the boat would be clearly seen from the air. He took *Mermaid* round in a wide sweep and throttled back the engines. 'Stand by your starboard anchor.' He held up his right hand when Ruth turned round. 'Four on deck, Mr Mate.' She waved. He slipped the engines out of gear and let the way run off as the boat headed into the stream. 'Let go.' Ruth leaned on the brake to start it then spun it off two turns. The chain roared over the gypsy then jerked to a stop as she checked it with the brake. Again. Check. Again, more chain this time. Check. A final run of chain. The brake screwed up tight. Four peals on the anchor bell. Smith switched off the engines and watched Ruth coming aft.

'Was that all right, sir?' she asked.

'Not bad. You forgot to wait and report when she was brought up.'

'I didn't forget. I don't even know what it means.'

'My fault then. It means the anchor's holding. It's not something that matters in the middle of a swamp.'

'Nothing matters now in the middle of a swamp.' She looked round at the river and up at the sky. 'Isn't it marvellous, Smithy? The air's different. Everything's different. *Mermaid*'s different. Like she was alive and kicking after being unconscious.' Her face was all joy, eyes bright, lips parted. 'You know, when I was up in the bows when we came out into the river I could've sworn the mermaid was laughing as the water sprayed over her and washed her clean and the bow wave crept up and teased the end of her tail.'

'Maybe she was laughing. She got herself a bath before we did.'

'A bath.' Ruth's eyes closed. She held them shut for a long time. 'Sorry, I was just trying to remember what a bath was like. I'd come to think that heaven was a half bucket of water and a sponge. Can I have a bath, Smithy?'

'Soon. I'm just going to start the pumps. If we give the tanks a bit of time to settle after we fill them, the water should be pretty clean. That'll give time for the heater to warm it through too.'

'That doesn't matter. I don't want hot water. Just water.

162

Lots of lovely cool clear water.' She frowned. 'No, you're right. Hot water. Lots of hot water. And cool water and cold water. And lots of soap and shampoo and everything.' She wet her lips. 'Can I have as much as I want? Can I run it and run it and run it?'

'Why not? I'm taking it out of the river. Will that be enough for you?'

She looked round. Upstream, downstream. 'I think so. Just.'

He grinned. 'Leave just a little for me. But before all that, there's this boat to make ship-shape.'

They worked on deck right through the heat of the day with only a short break for a snack. The heat seemed different out in the middle of the river. There seemed to be more air and it had a clean smell, not like the stench of decay that hovered over the swamp. The river helped, the sound of the running water competing for attention with the blistering sun. When all the gear was stowed Smith let Ruth go below for her bath. He knew that would take quite a while so he connected the deck hose and began washing down his boat.

He worked methodically, moving aft from the bows, directing the jet, chasing dirt and debris into the scuppers and over the side. Then he took the long-handled brush and scrubbed at the stubborn marks, oil, grease, mud, slime. Finally he honed the decks with the holystone and gave them another rinse with the hose. As the wood started to dry in the sun he could see that his decks were not perfect but they were starting to look like his decks. He went aft to start his last job. The funnel was still down. He had left it down till they were clear of the trees in the creek. He started polishing it, screwing up his eyes against the shine of the brass, regularly checking the empty sky. The helicopter was late.

Ruth stood under the shower and let the hot water cascade over her head and face and body. She kept thinking of Paradise and giggling at the thought that this really was the water of Paradise. She poured shampoo on to her hair and worked up a lather. She massaged her scalp till it tingled. Back under the shower. Then soap and her skin glowing with the scrubbing and the heat of the water. Next, cool water and her skin tightening as the pores closed up. Shower off, fill up the bath. She rubbed her hair and wrapped it in a towel as the water ran and steamed. Handfuls of bath salts and fragrance everywhere. She let herself slowly down into the hot water and stretched out. She moved her legs and watched the surface waves running and breaking on the side of the bath. She moved her arms and noticed the bulging muscles. She promised herself a rest from man's work. She let the heat seep into her flesh. She felt tired enough to sleep for a week. Wrapped in a towel she combed out her hair at the dressing-table in the main cabin. It was just like that first night. Even the cabin looked the same, the carpet and the furnishings all back in place, though showing signs of the flood. That first night. How long ago? Only a week? More like a lifetime.

Smith had just erected the funnel when she came on deck. He was patting it with one hand and giving it a final rub with a cloth in the other.

'You're just like a kid with that thing, Smithy.'

He had his back to her. He peered up its length. 'There's nothing wrong with kids. They've got beautifully simple priorities.' He turned and stared at her. His eyes moved over her from head to toe to head.

'Will you eat me now,' she asked, 'or will you wait till later?'

He laughed. 'Sorry. I'd forgotten.'

'It's nice you got your memory back.'

'I suppose so.' His eyes left her and searched the sky.

164

'You don't seem too sure.' She followed his gaze. 'What're you looking for?'

'The chopper.'

'Oh, maybe it won't come. It must know we'll be back in the river now.'

Smith shook his head. 'It'll come. It has to come.'

'Why must it come?'

He walked over close to her. 'It has to come because it's going to lift you off, Ruth.'

She frowned and shook her head. 'I don't understand, Smithy. What do you mean?'

'Just what I say. It's going to come and I'm going to signal it and it's going to send down a harness and you're going to put it on and be pulled up into the chopper and taken back to the capital.'

'Like hell I am.' Her voice was hard and determined.

'Ruth, it's the only way. I can't risk taking you down the river.'

'Smithy, I came on board to be taken to Port Bancourt. That's where I'm going. And I'm going in *Mermaid*. My fare's paid. I paid it with a week's hard labour over there in the swamp. No plane's lifting me anywhere.'

'All right, all right. Let's leave it be for now. The chopper's not here yet. Maybe you're right. Maybe it won't come.'

The sky stayed empty.

They ate properly that night. Smith cooked the meal and Ruth laid the saloon table with the best china and cutlery. The food was good but neither of them seemed to enjoy it. They tried lighthearted conversation but it died on them every time. When the coffee was poured and Smith had lit his cigar he broke the silence.

'We're both thinking about it, Ruth, so we might as well talk about it.' He blew on the end of his cigar and studied the ash. 'The chopper didn't come so we can assume it won't come tomorrow. That might mean anything but it probably means that Blik's waiting at the estuary. And that means that things could get a little rough.' He paused but Ruth said nothing. 'I can't risk anything happening to you so what I suggest is that we wait till the tribes come back, that shouldn't be long now, and I'll get them to take you across the swamp and through the hills and down to Port Bancourt. It won't be a nice trip but it'll be safe. Maybe you'll pick up a plane when you get in among the plantations. I'll give you a note. People know me.' He waited. 'Well, what d'you say?'

'I said it this afternoon. I'm going down the river with you.'

He pushed his cup across the table and got to his feet. 'What the hell's the matter with you, girlie? Does it run in your family, this need to go out and commit suicide?'

Her eyes flashed at him but her voice was controlled when she spoke. 'I know you too well now, Smithy. That one won't work.' She leaned on the table. 'But since you mention Jeth, let me say that you're more like him than I ever was. You're all the same, you men. Or maybe it's just that I'm a sucker for that kind of man. Yes, Jeth killed himself for a crazy idea. Just like you want to do. You're all the same, all hung up on a crazy code of so-called honour and manliness. Haven't you heard that the world you despise so much has outlawed duels to the death? Haven't you heard that nowadays life's about living not about dying? Haven't you heard that throwing down the gauntlet's the sign for sane people to take off to the hills? It's not new, you know. Turning the other cheek's at least two thousand years old. No, don't tell me. With you it's all about family. You and this orphan you picked up in the jungle. Haven't you heard about family, Smithy? That's all rubbish too. It doesn't mean a thing. It's just another prison like your fifteen million dollars' worth of gold. It's just a prison you let people build round you. And for why? Because by the merest chance one of your father's seeds happened to meet up with your mother's egg. Millions of sperms. Any other one and you wouldn't be here. There would never've been a you. As for you and Blik, you only need each other like a cripple needs crutches. Throw them away. Get up and walk. You've got a way out. You've just told me about it. Across the swamp and into the hills. No, you won't go that way, will you? That would mean leaving this precious boat of yours. That would mean giving up the only thing you really love. But you don't know about love. Love's about saving, love's about living, not about killing and dying.'

He stood and watched her. 'Quite a speech. Would I be right in thinking that you were trying to say that you're coming down the river with me tomorrow morning?'

'That's right. And I'll tell you something else. We're going to get to Port Bancourt. Nothing's going to happen. I know.'

'You know, do you. That'll be part of your crazy code, Ruth. Woman's intuition. That's what they call it, don't they?'

'You'll see.'

'I hope you're right. Believe me, I hope you're right.' He walked round and sat in his chair. He poured fresh coffee for both of them and drew on his cigar till it burned evenly again. He felt good. He'd give Blik a run for his money. Especially now. He listened to his boat. It whispered to him, its timbers settling themselves after their week-long torture, like a satisfied woman murmuring herself to sleep.

He turned his head as he caught a new sound. He got up and went over and stood at one of the screened windows, listening. He smiled. Then he laughed. He roared with laughter as he walked back and put a hand on Ruth's shoulder.

'What's the joke?' she asked angrily.

He threw his cigar in the ashtray and wiped his eyes. 'It's . . . it's the drums. D'you hear them? They . . . they must've heard you, Ruth. They . . . they're coming back, the tribes. They say, they say the danger's over.'

Chapter 13

The gunboat turned in a long slow arc and settled back on course. It had patrolled that ten mile beat of sea, up and down, to and fro, since early morning the day before. It was now afternoon. The little warship was three miles off the coast, beyond the maze of mudbanks that sealed off the Paradise to all but the foolhardy and Smith. More so now since the flood. Each low tide laid bare the quick mud. The charts had never been exact but now they were a mockery. The officers had checked at low water. The flood had changed the channels, shifted the banks, scoured out here, piled up there. Anyone who thought he knew the estuary was in for a shock.

President Blik walked across the open bridge under the awning and leaned on the starboard rail. It was high tide, the mudbanks covered. There was smooth water all the way in to the coast, tempting but treacherous. Mist clung to the surface in dense patches, hardly moving in the hot still air. Mist that came with each high tide and the meeting of sea and river, mist that shut out vision through it but opened long vistas of empty water in the spaces in between. The radar scanner scythed relentlessly up above, probing out to sea and up into the river, painting its monotonous picture on the screen, an outline of land and jungle, of mudbanks when uncovered, an occasional target on the blank spaces that were water, something to rouse the operator for a moment, but always a false alarm, the ripped off roof of a native hut, a huge tree, its branches still leafed, also-rans in the deluge of destruction wrought by the flood. Never a firm, unmistakable moving target. No sign of *Mermaid*.

169

Come on, Smiddy. Where are you? What's happened? You know I'm here. Let's get on with it. Don't let me down again. Don't chicken out. Blik was hot and tired. He had slept badly on the overnight run to the estuary but anticipation had kept him alert all through that day. That and worry that he might have missed Smith. He had thought that through and made himself realise it was impossible. He had left the capital as soon as he had Loder's report. An hour before that, *Mermaid* was still high and dry. The gunboat was off the estuary before dawn. Not even Smith could have launched the boat and brought it down the river and through the mudbanks in darkness. Or could he? No, there must be another explanation. All through the second night Blik had weighed the evidence, trying to put himself in Smith's place, planning the moves, finding the snags, changing the moves. He had slept hardly at all. Now another day was slipping past. He stared at the mist teasing itself into weird shapes over the water. He moistened his lips. What's happened, Smiddy? Are you stuck up there in your Paradise? Did your engines fail to start? Is something else wrong? Or did you start down and run aground? Take your time. I'll wait for you. You haven't cut and run. I'm sure of that. You haven't left your precious boat and crept away across the swamp. Not unless you've changed. Maybe you have changed. It's been a long time. No, I know what's happened. You waited till yesterday to launch *Mermaid*. That was the sensible thing to do. Then you'd have to test everything, get everything working, probably scrub down and polish all the brass. That's the you I remember. Then last night you'd sit there all alone in the saloon and eat a good meal and smoke a cigar and think about today. I wonder what you thought. You'll have a plan, several. You won't just come down here and stick your head in the noose. You'll want me to try and you'll hope I fail. That way you'll have won. But I won't fail. I had a good teacher. I've got good cause too. All that gold. Why, Smiddy? You, the one incorruptible man I've ever known. I wonder how you feel now about your fat accounts in Zurich or Geneva or wherever you put it all. It can't have been worth it. It's bought you death. From me of all people. Come on, Smiddy. Let's get it over with.

A telephone buzzed on the bridge. Blik looked round. The officer of the watch answered it. He nodded and hooked up the phone. Blik sighed and turned back to his vigil. Then the commander was at his side. They had a target. This time it was definite. Still up in the river but on course downstream.

Blik dried his palms on his shirt and lifted the binoculars. The tide had turned. The ebb was starting and the patches of mist writhed over the moving water. He trained the glasses on the coast, then round to the mouth of the Paradise. Mist shut out the view, then opened a long sight up the river. The glasses tracked and stopped. There. A low white profile, almost broadside on from where the gunboat was. An undistinguished profile at that distance but for the gleaming column of the funnel, winking like a heliograph in the afternoon sun.

A klaxon squawked through the gunboat, shattering the quiet, stirring up a frenzy of warlike sounds.

*   *   *

Smith saw the mist on the mudbanks. That's good. Just what I expected. That might give me a little extra time. If I need it. If you're there, Blik. Just enough time to pick out the right channel, if there are any channels. There's a thought. Crazy thought. There must be a way through. Even if the flood stopped them all up, in a week the river must have cut new ways through. But maybe only at high water. I've chosen the ebb.

He had chosen the ebb for many reasons. With the ebb

171

running, the banks would start to show and that would be a fair guide to where the channels lay. With the ebb running the tide would be with him so his speed would be higher if full power was needed. With the ebb running, Blik's gunboat, if it was there, would have to stand well out to sea. That would give Smith room. And the timing was right. The ebb would run on till it was dark. If Smith could make it to the sea as darkness fell, nothing would catch him.

The river was broadening every moment now as *Mermaid* ran down towards the estuary. Smith held her out into mid-river. From there he would be able to scan the whole spread of the mudbanks as they started to uncover, to guess at the channels, to pick the best route, to avoid the chance of being trapped close to the shore. He had fought the coming battle a dozen times that day already as he brought his boat slowly and carefully down the Paradise but he knew that when it happened, if it happened, it would not run according to any plan. Success would depend on his keen eye and his instinct for survival. All that and a large measure of luck. The oil drums lined up along the rail on both sides of the boat were proof of Smith's belief that luck favoured those who wanted to win and worked at shortening the odds.

This was one battle Smith wanted desperately to win. He sensed the reasons were new. The importance of his long separation from Blik and the chance to solve it once for all had faded. There were no longer just the two of them. Ruth stood between them. Her safety was more important. So why bring her down the river? You could've stayed up there. You could've taken her across the swamp and into the hills. You could've waited till the tribes came back and got them to take her across. What's the matter, Smithy? D'you need someone to hold your hand? Tell yourself the truth. You've caught a bad case of old man's fantasies. You're starting to believe what she says, that nothing's going to

172

happen, that Blik's not there, that it's all your imagination. That could turn out to be a fatal disease, Smithy. For both of you. Maybe so. Then maybe not. Look ahead there. D'you see Blik? No, you don't. The estuary's empty. Maybe she is right, maybe we'll have a clear run through to Port Bancourt. Then what? D'you think she'll creep into that big bed and say Thank You? You are getting old, Smithy. She'll be off back to her world, to young people and fun and life. What's wrong with that? She came on board to go to Port Bancourt. I just want to see her safely there. Ha, ha, bloody ha. You old liar. You're just a randy old man trying to kid yourself you're doing the big uncle bit. Why don't you give up? Your last attempt at adoption got you where you are now, all screwed up and waiting for your son to blow you and your boat out of the water. And Ruth Carter with it. There's still time. Turn back up the Paradise. Be a man, Smithy, and run scared for once. Tell her now. Here she is with a big glass of juice to wet your dry throat.

Smith took the glass and sipped the cold juice. He said nothing. The ebb was starting to run. The shape of one mudbank was already showing ahead. Once into the channels he would be committed. There would be no turning back. He drained the glass and gave it to Ruth. He gripped the wheel and swept his eyes across the water. He picked out the little ruffles that came from the breeze blowing offshore. Another plus. That could help. He checked the sun, starting to drop steeply in the west. Good again. That sun would be facing anyone lying offshore. And less than an hour till it set and started the quick darkness. The pattern of the banks was starting to show clearly. Just what I thought. Lots of changes. That big one in the middle looks good. Branches out on both sides farther out. That's the one. There's still time, Smithy. You're not committed yet. Turn round and run. It's too big a chance. Aw, shut up and let me get on with it. He gripped the wheel and steadied

173

Mermaid on course for the main channel.

Ruth stood beside him in the wheelhouse. Her confidence that nothing would happen had waned steadily as they came down the river. She had fought against it, telling herself that all the signs were on her side; the empty river, the birds in the trees and in the air and on the water, the clear sky, the blazing sun and the boat's unhindered progress downstream. But it was all unreal after her week in the swamp. It was like the calm before the storm. Smith too seemed calm and in control but his concentration, his alertness, fed her doubts. That was silly. Of course he was alert. He had to be. The flood had changed the bed of the river, dumped wreckage that was still breaking free and floating away on the current. He had to be alert, to concentrate, just to get them safely out of the Paradise. But there was more to it than that. She had not convinced him. He was waiting for Blik to make a move. He had given her another chance in the early morning to change her mind, to stay upriver and wait for the tribes. He had been brutally frank. He had told her that going with him might mean she'd be dead before sunset. She squinted up at the sun. Not long. She felt the sweat on her face and on her back, running and soaking the waistband of her slacks. She felt the sweat on her hands and rubbed them dry on her clothes. She shivered as she looked ahead and saw the mud uncovering with the ebb. It was as if the estuary was unsheathing its claws. Her stomach ached. So this was what real fear was like, the fear soldiers knew going into battle, fear of the unknown, fear of the beautiful landscape that hid the engines of death. Ruth was of a generation that turned its back on war, that condemned the kind of code that drove men like Smith to stake his life for what he thought was right. She still thought it wrong, she still saw life through younger eyes but she knew she was there on that boat because he was there. When she looked at him, when she thought of him, she was sucked into a maelstrom of conflicting feelings; awe, disgust, anger, affection, admiration, contempt. And desire. Her girlish ideal. A physical man with a brain. She had known since they fought in the swamp. She had wanted him then. She had hated him for rejecting her and loved him for why. She looked out ahead across the estuary and shivered again as she saw the unlikely mist on that tropic sea, opening and shutting, swirling into grotesque and threatening shapes.

Smith slowed the engines as *Mermaid* slid into the main channel. He switched on the echo sounder and watched the red neon as it winked on the dial, spelling out the depth. His eyes searched the water ahead, watching each ripple and eddy, translating them into contours of mud under the surface. His eyes flicked up to the patches of mist retreating with the tide, breaking up, dissipating. What was that? It was gone behind the mist. A ship or just a shadow? Blik's gunboat or a swooping bird? Nothing. Just mist. He moved the wheel to hold the middle of the channel. The echo sounder showed plenty of water. He searched the estuary for a route. That looked likely. A channel branching to port, bending back towards the coast then connecting with another channel parallel to the shore. That was the route if nothing happened. That would take him towards the sea on the British side. If the channels all led to new channels. If they were deep enough. If he made no mistakes. If nothing happened. If Blik wasn't somewhere out there. If Ruth was right and he was wrong. An awful lot of ifs.

It started suddenly. A wide break in the mist, the gunboat broadside on about four miles and wide on the starboard bow. A puff and flash from the gun on its foredeck, then the scream of a shell. Smith's hand on Ruth's shoulder, dropping her to her knees, his voice loud and harsh through the sound of the shell. 'Get down and stay down.' His left hand on the wheel, the right hovering over the control panel, touching nothing, leaving the engines slowed down, waiting to spot the shell, searching ahead, juggling plans. The scream cut off as the shell burst, the noise muffled by the water and mud thrown into the air. Too long and off line. Two hundred yards away on the port bow. 'Come on, Blik,' yelled Smith. 'You can do better than that. Throw the next one short and try for a bracket.'

Ruth was on her knees, shouting. 'Stop, Smithy. For God's sake, stop. Give up. Stop.'

He took no notice of her, revved the engines to half speed and held his course. His eyes moved from the gunboat to the channel ahead to the channel to starboard. That was the one. Turn there and head straight at the gunboat. Reduce the target. Fox the gunners by closing not running. Wink and puff. The scream of the shell less strident, dropping short. 'That's it, Blik. Just what I wanted.' He pushed the throttles wide open and *Mermaid* surged ahead, her stern squatting, her bow lifting. The shell exploded at the far end of the starboard channel, throwing up a column of water, obscuring the gunboat. 'Thanks, Blik.' He spun the wheel and the boat heeled as it clawed to starboard and into the branch channel. Midships. Steady. The shell's spray had subsided. The boat was heading straight at the warship.

Smith hauled Ruth to her feet. 'Hold her so.' He put her hands on the wheel and ran out on to the deck. He lifted a can of petrol and sprayed it over the open oil drums. A big windproof match into each drum, a roar of flames, dying quickly, streamers of smoke as the oily waste ignited, streamers growing to billowing clouds. Smith was back in the wheelhouse, pushing Ruth out of the way. 'I'll take her.' The boat was racing for the end of the channel. Puff and flash, the shriek of the shell overhead, the thump and gush as it hit the mud on the edge of the main channel. Smith was laughing. Hard a starboard. Full astern starboard engine. The boat canted and seemed to skid ahead through the water as it turned. Full astern port. She was almost round. All stop. She was round and heading back the way she had come. Full ahead both. 'Take her now. Just so.' Ruth gripped the wheel and stared ahead. The water was still frothed and stained with the last shell burst. Smith was out on deck heaving the drums over the side. One. Two. Three. Four. Five. He was back at the wheel, his face streaming with sweat and streaked from the black smoke. His grin was wide but tight, fierce, and his eyes blazed with the mad light of battle. Another shell howled, an octave lower, short. But the line was good. It hit the water dead astern at fifty yards. 'That's better, Blik. Now try on that smoke for size.'

The drums were astern, bobbing in ragged line ahead, caught by the ebb, drifting into the maze of small channels, always seawards and belching out thick black smoke. The offshore breeze was laying the smoke on the water, teasing it out, stretching a black screen between hunter and hunted.

The gunboat was out of sight, blinded. But the next shell was perilously close, screaming in and bursting in the mud only thirty yards on the starboard bow. Mud showered down on the boat. 'You're getting lucky, Blik boy.' They were back at the junction with the main channel. Hard a port. Back up towards the Paradise. That'll fool them. Steady now. Look for that first channel, the one that led off and inshore. Blik won't expect that. He'll guess I'll try and work to seaward. Smith laughed as a shell wailed hopelessly in search of a target and burst a quarter of a mile astern. 'I can read you like a book, you bastard.'

Starboard now into that other channel, slow down, take

it easy, watch the depth, find the right way, make no mistakes. That's it. Come on, my beauty. We'll do it. We're winning.

The quiet was unexpected, unreal, just the running water and the throb of the engines. The smoke still lay on the water but it was thinning. Let's fix that. He slowed the engines right down and called to Ruth. 'Take her again.' There was no answer. He looked round. Ruth was standing in the corner of the wheelhouse, staring ahead. She seemed dazed. He stretched out and grabbed her arm. 'Come on, come on, it's not over yet.'

Her head jerked round and she stared at him as if he was a stranger. She let him pull her behind the wheel and put her hands on the spokes.

'Have you got her? Just so.'

She nodded and blinked her eyes.

He ran out and lit five more drums on the other side of the deck. He stood back as the petrol flared then dropped them one at a time over the side, trying to feed them into one of the seaward channels. Three ran true on the current, the others stayed alongside and missed the opening. A shell made up Smith's mind. It whined overhead and burst on the shore. He ran back inside and took the wheel, pushing the throttles wide open. The chase was on again. 'That's better, Blik boy. Using your radar, are you? You're learning.' *Mermaid*'s bow was up under full power, her wake chasing her as it rushed along the edge of the mudbanks now high on both sides. Smith's eyes searched ahead, picking the deepest water, his hands guiding the boat in its race for the open sea. Shells screamed and landed and burst, ahead, astern, over, short, the gunners firing blind but for the ranges and bearings from the radar, the operator straining to keep track of the racing target half-hidden by the rising mud left behind by the ebbing tide. The new smoke was well laid, overlapping the reach of the first screen, stretching a new pall as the warship sped at full power round the seaward limit of the estuary. The sun was dropping quickly, already shut off from view behind the land. Not long till dusk and then the sudden darkness.

Starboard easy. That's my girl. Round this bend and you're on the home stretch. Easy now. Smith's stomach knotted as he felt the lift in his feet. Damn and blast. She's hit the mud. He felt the lift and heel as the starboard keel dug in. Port wheel. Keep on full power. Pray. The boat hesitated, struggled, shuddered, slid free. The bow rose and she leapt ahead again. Wow. Near thing. Watch it, Smithy. A shell burst thirty yards ahead and the boat was in the spray before it settled. 'Thanks, Blik. You got the range right. You won't do that again in a hurry.'

There it is, the open sea and the cape. Maybe ten minutes. The channel was straight for the next mile, parallel to the coast, the water deepening now, safer, the mudbanks less exposed, more dangerous. A shell shrieked over astern and exploded on the beach. 'Watch it, Blik boy. You're hitting British sand there.' Less than ten minutes, dusk, the open sea and the cape. Not even Blik would risk a shell on the other side of that cape.

The scream was different, close, stunning, frightening. Was this a shell on target, a direct hit? Not a shell. The engines. The port engine. An engine without a screw. A severed shaft revving madly with no propeller to take its power. Gears howled as they raced beyond endurance. The port shaft, the one that had been bent in the swamp, the one Smith had heated and hammered and straightened. Just two seconds. Smith threw the engine out of gear and wound on starboard wheel, slowed the good engine. Too late. The channel was narrow. With the port screw gone, its mate took over the boat. The bow swept to port and, even as Smith corrected, *Mermaid* hit the mud underwater, her speed pushing her into and up on the bank, the impact throwing Ruth across the wheelhouse and bending Smith over the wheel. A long-drawn shudder as the boat was trapped and held. Smith came erect and pulled the one engine to full astern. But he knew it was hopeless. She had taken the mud at full speed. With the ebb still running, every second meant less water and more mud. She was stuck fast. Within sight of freedom but now without a chance. *Mermaid* was a sitting target.

Chapter 14

Max Haltone was a mild-mannered man, easy going, but with an unexpected streak of determination that nearly always got him what he was after. He was in Mr Soong's office in Government House.

'I'm sorry, Professor, you cannot see the president because he's not in the capital. He's away directing relief work following the flood.' The Chinaman paused. 'The president did assure the American authorities that your request would have immediate attention when conditions made travel possible.'

'Yes, yes. I know. But I've been here for ten days now. I can't wait for ever. I've got important work to do and I can't do it here. How long d'you think till I can travel? Tomorrow? The next day? You must have some idea.'

'None at all, Professor. I am sorry. But maybe not too long.'

'I hope so. I'm a patient man, Mr Soong. But I don't like being stalled. I like to know how things stand.'

'Do you think that the president is stalling, as you put it? Surely not, Professor. President Blik would be very upset to hear that you thought that. You have been told of the lava flow on the mountain, you know about the flood caused by the emptying of the lake, surely you've read of all the destruction. I'm sure you can guess at the administrative problems that has caused in a country with our poor facilities.'

'Yes, I suppose so. I guess I'll just have to wait. But it's not easy, Mr Soong. This isn't my favourite town.'

'I am sorry.'

Haltone turned away, then stopped and peered at a tray on Soong's desk. 'That's interesting,' he said, scooping up the pile of photos and shuffling through them. He smiled at the Chinaman. 'You don't mind, do you? Not state secrets, I hope.' He turned his eyes back to the photos. 'Very interesting. A ship in the middle of the jungle.' He peered. 'Sort of swamp, it looks like.' He leafed through the prints. 'Very, very interesting.' He put a hand into his pocket and pulled out a folding glass. He held it up and inspected the photos. 'Clever. Very clever. Tree trunks under the boat, wires, no, anchor chains leading out in front. Heave on chains and boat moves. Very clever.' He stepped back in front of Soong. 'You don't mind? Hobby of mine, aerial survey. Part of my job really. I use it to find likely sites for my excavations. These are great pictures.'

Soong smiled and held out his hand. 'Yes, they are good. One of your American pilots took them. The ship was stranded by the flood. We could do nothing to help, just watch. As you can see, Captain Smith's a very resourceful man.'

'He sure is. See here. He's right back near the water. Looks small for a river though. That Paradise River of yours is broader than that.'

'Yes, that's a creek that runs into the river.'

'Amazing. Fascinating.'

Soong's hand was still out, waiting for the prints. 'Yes, very remarkable. It is difficult to believe that one man could move that ship that distance all by himself.'

'Well, let's be exact. Not quite by himself. There were at least two of them.'

'No, just one. Just Captain Smith.'

'I'm sorry, Mr Soong, you're wrong this time. See here, on this one, one on the ground and another up there on the bow, I suppose it is, there under that sort of shade thing.'

182

'You must be wrong, Professor.' Soong was on his feet.

'I'm not wrong, Mr Soong. I'm an expert at this. Here, wait, there's a zoom shot here somewhere.' He shuffled the photos. 'This one. Look here. One on the ground and another up on the boat.' He trained his glass. 'Yes, one on the ground and anoth . . .' He looked up at Soong and his face was suddenly pale, eyes angry, mouth tight. 'What the hell's going on? That's my Ruth on that boat, Soong. The Ruth Carter I came to see. She's supposed to be up in that valley, up on the mountain, with the Pochaks. What the hell's going on here?'

Soong pulled the photos from his hand. 'There's no need to worry, Professor. I'm sure you're mistaken. But if Miss Carter is with Captain Smith, she'll be quite safe.'

'I'm not mistaken, Soong. I want to know what's going on.' He followed Soong as the Chinaman backed towards Blik's office. 'I've been stalled along for ten days now. I want to know about Ruth Carter. I warn you. . .'

'Everything will be all right, Professor. Don't worry. Excuse me, that's the phone in the president's office.'

'I heard nothing. Now look here . . .'

'Yes, the phone. Excuse me.' He opened the door, slipped through and slammed it. He turned the key. Don't worry. She'll be quite safe with Captain Smith. He shook his head and hurried to the desk. The room echoed to Haltone's fist beating on the door. Soong picked up the private phone and dialled the special number.

* * *

Blik had enjoyed the hunt. With that first sighting of *Mermaid*, all his tiredness had fallen away. He had known it would not be quick. He knew Smith and he knew his own little navy. He had every confidence they would not hit the boat at any kind of distance. He had seen the gunners at practice. The hunt would go on till they trapped Smith's boat and ran in close. The smoke delighted him. Good, Smiddy. You're fighting. You're going to make it worth while.

He panicked when he saw the denseness of the smoke and the way it was stretching out on the water. What're you up to behind there, Smiddy? Making for the sea? Backtracking? That's more like it. Backtracking and searching for a way out along the British coast towards the cape. He ordered full speed and told the commander to round the banks as close as he dare. Good, a radar contact. So I was right, Smiddy. Keep at it. Keep running. Now I know where you are, I'll hold my fire till I see you again. Damn you. Damn you, you old fox. More smoke. You're even better than I remember. Open fire again. Range and bearing by radar.

The gunboat was shaking from end to end with her engines at full power. Blik gripped the bridge rail and stared into the drifting smoke, wincing each time the gun roared, wanting to see the fall of shot, worried at the chance of missing the kill. He listened to the radar reports on the intercom. Smith was also at full speed, even faster with the ebb tide under him. The radar kept losing him between the mudbanks. I've got to hand it to you, Smiddy. You've still got what it takes. You haven't changed. But you have changed. That's why I'm going to kill you. You have changed, haven't you? Blik turned his eyes ahead to the cape. Are we fast enough? Can we catch him? We mustn't lose him. He mustn't get away. Can't this old rattle-trap move faster? No target on radar. Correction. Target stationary. Rubbish. Check that. Confirmation. Target is stationary.

Got you, Smiddy. You've made a mistake, haven't you? You've hit the mud. Got you. You gave me a good run. I'll give you that. Just let that smoke clear and I'll give you your prize. In person. Would you like that? I'll go down and lay and train that gun, then pull the lanyard. Is that fair, Smiddy?

The commander was beside him. Government House was on the R/T. Tell them to wait. It was very, very urgent. Damn. He went over and picked up the phone. He was looking ahead. They had just run clear of the smoke. He could see *Mermaid*, stern on, trapped, helpless. He heard Soong's voice. He jerked up his head and yelled at the top of his voice. 'Hold your fire.' The gun roared before the words were all out. Blik dropped the phone and listened to the swish of the shell going away. It was not far. A second or two. Smith's boat disappeared in a cascade of mud and water.

'You bloody fool. I told you to hold your fire. There's been a mistake. That's the wrong target.'

'Near miss,' reported the spotter.

Blik looked up. It was true. *Mermaid* was still there. He put up his glasses. No sign of life. But there wouldn't be. You'll be crouched down somewhere in there and safe, Smiddy. Funny. All these years but I know I'd know if you were dead. You're alive and you're off the hook. I can't touch you now, not with that American on board. A woman. I might have known. How is it with her, Smiddy? Have you had her into that big bed yet?

He lowered the glasses and told the commander to stand down the men. Have to give that a bit of thought. Have to think up a good story for the commander. He kept his eyes on *Mermaid*. Now I'll never know if I could have killed you, Smiddy. Not having done it, I'll have to go on wondering whether I should've. Funny. I'm glad I didn't. I'm free of you now. You won't ever risk it back up the Paradise. What'll you do? Leave the island, go and spend all that gold money? You did take that gold. That I know. Now I'll never be sure why. Now I'll never be sure what you did with it. Blik smiled slowly. And you'll never know why I didn't kill you. Be kind to that Ruth Carter, Smiddy. She just saved your life.

*   *   *

Smith kept the starboard engine running astern long after he knew there was no hope of breaking free. He was stunned at being beaten. It had all seemed so certain.

Ruth struggled to her feet. 'What . . . what happened?'

He came to at the sound of her voice. He cut the engine and all noise died but for the small sounds of running water and sucking mud. 'We threw a propeller. Something like that. We're up on the mud. Fast. I'm sorry.'

Through the side window he saw the gunboat steaming clear of the smoke. He watched it. There was nothing to do. It was all inevitable now. The belch of smoke and the flash from the gun broke his trance. He grabbed Ruth and dragged her to the deck, covering her with his body as the shell screamed in and hit and exploded only yards from the port quarter. *Mermaid* bucked and shifted on the mud. Shrapnel thudded into her superstructure and whined off her iron hull. Mud and water rained down on her. They lay together on the deck, quite still. Smith felt empty, already dead. Something of his old self stirred deep in his brain, urging him to fight, telling him it wasn't all over, that there was still time. But he knew there was no time. He knew the gunboat was out there, clear of his smoke, not more than two miles off. It was hard to lose but it would never happen again. This time was for keeps. He lay still, his body over Ruth's in a useless gesture of protection, his face buried in her hair.

A minute. Three minutes. Five minutes.

He lifted his head slowly, blinking his eyes as if waking from sleep. He saw the sky up through the side window, its pale brilliant blue already a darker shade, deepening as he watched. He pushed himself to his knees and looked through the window. The gunboat was there, its bow wave small, slowed down, heading for the cape. Smith got to his feet and moved to the open doorway of the wheelhouse. He watched the warship turn slowly and steam back on the opposite course. You're a sweet bastard, Blik. You've changed. Stretching out the agony, that's not the you I knew. He jumped through the door to the rail and yelled at the gunboat. 'Here I am, Blik. Get it over with. One shot. That's all you need. Come on. Kill me.' He watched and waited. Nothing. No puff of smoke, no flash of fire. Just the gunboat steaming slowly on the sea. He looked up at the sky, then west, east. Dusk was settling in. Already detail was fuzzed. Smith's eyes narrowed. What's happened? What's it all about? Have you run out of guts, Blik? Are you having your after-kill remorse before the kill? Or has that clapped out old gun fallen to bits on you? Never mind what, you're giving me a chance. You should know better than that, Blik boy. One chance is all I need.

He ran back into the den and grabbed a pad and pencil. Ruth was sitting up, staring, bewildered. 'You stay right there. Don't move.' He ran out and leapt up the ladder to the monkey island. He pulled off the binnacle cover and spun the bearing plate, sighting across the compass, scribbling figures, swivelling the plate and sighting again. The warship was already a hazed shape on the sea. He waited till the dusk was almost darkness then climbed down to the wheelhouse. Ruth was still where he had left her.

'Hope you're all right in the dark,' he said. 'I don't want to show any lights.'

Her voice was uncertain, slow as if she was fighting to control it. 'That's good, isn't it? The darkness.'

'Could be.' Smith was too close to the past quarter-hour to make predictions.

'Can I get up now?'

'Yes, if you want. What do you plan to do without any

lights?' He gave her his hand and helped her up.

'I . . . I don't plan to do anything except find out if my legs are there and if I can stand on them.'

'They are and you can.' He let her go. 'I didn't have the chance before so thanks for all your help. We'd never even have got this far without you to take the wheel.'

'That was nothing. You did it all.'

'Well, that's us both thanked. D'you happen to know any good games to play in the dark, Miss Carter? We've got a long wait.'

'What for? Isn't it over? What happened anyway? Was it just the darkness that saved us?'

'No, Ruth, it wasn't the darkness. But the dark's important. It gives us another chance.'

She felt her way to the door and stared out at the hidden sea. 'Why, Smithy? How?'

'We'll never know for sure. Maybe that gun packed up. It's a beat-up little ship. Something like that, some technical problem.'

'Maybe Blik just couldn't do it in the end. Maybe he never meant to kill you, just scare you.'

'He certainly did that. No, he meant it. These weren't tennis balls he was lobbing at us. But something stopped him. What's not important.'

'Has he gone? Is it all over?'

'That's something else we don't know. He's maybe out there now. He's maybe trying to put things right before dawn. He's maybe going to send in a boat on the flood tide. There's a thought.' Smith groped his way across the wheelhouse and checked his rifles.

'What are you doing, Smithy?'

'Taking precautions.'

Ruth shivered in the cold darkness. She never wanted to see a gun or hear a shot again. She was barely out of the nightmare of the afternoon till it seemed to be starting up

188

again, worse now because of the dark. 'If he has gone, what happens to us?'

'Whether he's gone or not, we hope the tide lifts us off this mud.'

'And if it doesn't?'

'It better. I can get her off in daylight with the anchors but I don't fancy taking the chance of waiting till then. So pray for a good tide.'

They sat in the darkness in Smith's den. The ebb ran out, the tide stood still, then the water started flooding back up the channels, filling them, starting to submerge the banks. They used a shielded torch to see to make some food and brew coffee. There was no talk. It was as if talk was irrelevant till they knew if *Mermaid* would break free. Smith went out and checked the rising water from time to time. He said nothing but he was worried about how hard the boat had gone aground. It was the time of the neap tides with a low high water. It might not be enough to lift the boat off. He sat in the den and sipped coffee and worried at the problem.

His chuckle sounded loud in the still darkness. It grew into a suppressed laugh. Ruth could feel the settee vibrating as Smith's mirth shook his body.

'Can I share the joke?' she asked.

He tried to catch his breath. 'Yes . . . yes . . . of course.' He was taken by a fit of laughter.

Sitting in the darkness, seeing only his vague shape against the tiny light filtering in from the stars, she imagined the tears streaming down his cheeks. It sounded like that kind of laughter. 'Come on then, Smithy. Tell me.'

He lay back against the cushion and gasped. Then he got up. 'Can you remember how to work that windlass, Ruth?'

'How could I forget?'

'Good girl. On your feet then. Take my hand. I'll lead.'

'Wait a minute. What about the windlass? Are we going to pull *Mermaid* off with the anchors after all? Is that the joke?'

'No.' He started to laugh again but suppressed it. 'Not with the anchors. With the derrick.'

'Smithy, I don't understand.'

'You will,' he told her. 'We're going to dump the ballast.'

She stood quite still. She had forgotten all about the gold. She was dazed. Smith was right. It was funny. Excruciatingly funny. He had found a good cause. He had discovered something worth buying. She took a deep breath. 'What are we waiting for, Captain?'

She started the windlass and ran it slowly as Smith topped the derrick and stripped the hatch covers. She stood up there breathing the cool night air, watching the shadows thrown up from the hold as Smith worked by the light of a torch. It was a long wait but she felt no impatience. He came on deck and she wound the runner wire on to the drum and the cargo tray rose out of the hold. Smith hauled on the guy and the derrick swung away and hung over the mud. He took hold of the heaving line he had tied in a slip to two of the tray's legs. He gave a sharp pull and one side dropped. A king's ransom in ballast cascaded into the mud, splashed, slid and sank out of sight with greedy gurglings. Three more loads and all the fifteen million dollars' worth of gold were buried deep in the quick mud of the estuary.

By then the rising tide had covered the bank and there was water all round the boat. Smith started the one engine and with it and the rudder he swung the stern first one way then the other to help the boat break free. She came off half an hour before high water, sliding back into the channel, at once coming alive as she felt the tide.

Smith settled down behind the wheel, his eyes on the

compass, keeping the course he had calculated in these few minutes before dark, using a lot of rudder to compensate for the missing propeller. The red neon on the echo sounder marked the depth, showing they were moving all the time into deeper water.

Ruth stood beside him as he coaxed *Mermaid* along the channel, watched as he edged her round one bend, then another. She saw the half moon rise and throw its white light across the water. The sea was empty. There was no sign of Blik's gunboat. She looked back at the island. Even at that great distance the mountain showed, a great truncated pyramid against the sky, edged with a collar of white and crowned by a red mist. A long way, a long time. She remembered it all. Dear Jethro, the wonderful Pochaks, that beautiful valley. She turned back to Smith. He was standing straight, relaxed.

'Have we reached the sea?' she asked.

'As good as.'

'Tell me that story now, Smithy. You promised.'

He looked round then back up ahead. 'What story? What promise?'

'That first day we met. When I gave you Pagotak's message. You remember the one. Saying he hoped you'd now feel his debt was paid. You promised to tell me about it if we reached the sea.'

'So I did.' He chuckled. 'It's an old Pochak custom. If someone saves your life, you're in his debt and, as a warrior, you must repay that debt. Even if it takes you the rest of your life, even if you have to give up your most valuable possessions. Pogostick thought I saved his life once during the war.'

'Go on.'

'That's all. End of story.'

'But how did Pagotak settle his debt?'

'Well, he used the usual Pochak way.' Smith paused. 'He offered his best woman in settlement. Sort of a wife for a life.'

'I see. And did you accept?'

'Not right away. Just at the time I had rather a lot on my mind. But I think maybe I will now. He's a nice fellow. It's a long time. I don't see why he should stay in debt all his life. How do you feel about that, Ruth?'

She moved a little closer, till their arms touched. 'I feel fine, Smithy. Just fine.'